TWELFTH NIGHT

TWELFTH NIGHT

WILLIAM SHAKESPEARE

ILLUSTRATED BY

W. HEATH ROBINSON

LEOPARD

This edition published in Great Britain
in 1995 by Leopard Books,
Random House, 20 Vauxhall Bridge Road,
London SW1V 2SA

Published in the USA
in 1994 by Gramercy Books

Grateful acknowledgement is made to
George Weidenfeld & Nicholson Ltd,
for permission to reprint the text used in this edition,
originally published in
The New Temple Shakespeare series,
edited by M. R. Ridley.

Designed by Melissa Ring

ISBN 0 7529 0099 4

Printed and bound in Singapore

8 7 6 5 4 3 2 1

PREFACE

Twelfth Night, or *What You Will*, was probably written around 1600. In many ways it is the culmination of Shakespeare's earlier comedies. From his *Comedy of Errors* he borrows the concept of twins wreaking havoc because of mistaken identity. From *As You Like It* he takes the idea of a heroine disguising herself as a boy. In his earlier comedies, Shakespeare seems to be exploring the purely entertaining aspects of farce, but *Twelfth Night* has a darker undercurrent that adds a new dimension to the realm of Shakespearean comedy.

The plan conveys a festive atmosphere. By calling it *Twelfth Night* Shakespeare is clearly alluding to the feast of Epiphany, which was once an important Christian holiday that also marked the end of the Christmas season. By Shakespeare's day, however, it had devolved into a period of holiday abandon during which the usual restraints and conventions of everyday life were put aside and disorder ruled. This is the ambience of the play. The character of Sir Toby Belch, who never emerges from inebriated revelry, seems to be the guiding spirit. Illyria, where the play is set, seems a topsy-turvy world. When Viola is shipwrecked here she believes she has lost her twin brother, Sebastian. She disguises herself as a boy and begins to work for the Duke Orsino, who insists that she woo the noble lady Olivia on his behalf. Of course Olivia falls in love with Viola, and, to complicate matters, Sebastian is still alive. Chaos ensues as mistaken identity creates even more confusion.

Twelfth Night ends with the marriages that usually concluded Shakespeare's comedies. This signalled to his audience a symbolic return to the natural order of life. But the play leaves some issues unresolved. Foremost is the case of Malvolio, Olivia's dour and serious steward. Through the mischievous manipulations of Sir Toby and his minions of misrule, Malvolio accepts the preposterous idea that Olivia, his employer, is in love with him. Although the situation is funny, by the end of the play, after Malvolio has been imprisoned and stripped of all self-respect and dignity, the joke has gone too far. During the concluding nuptial betrothals, Malvolio's "I'll be reveng'd on the whole pack of you" strikes a disquieting note, a touch of tragic reality amidst an otherwise fairy-tale conclusion. *Twelfth Night* clearly points toward Shakespeare's later, even more troubling comedy, *Measure for Measure*, and his final tragicomedies.

Many of Shakespeare's plays were first published individually in Quarto editions that were later collected and published in Folio editions. But the only source for *Twelfth Night* is the First Folio edition of 1623. It is this edition that is reprinted in this book, and it is the nearest possible approximation to what Shakespeare actually wrote. To avoid distraction, however, the spelling has been modernized. The punctuation adheres closely to the Elizabethan punctuation of the early text and, therefore, is often indicative of the way in which the lines are to be spoken.

   This handsome edition of *Twelfth Night* is illustrated by W. Heath Robinson, who artfully captures the merrymaking and abandon of the play.

CHRISTOPHER MOORE

New York
1994

DRAMATIS PERSONAE

ORSINO, *Duke of Illyria.*
SEBASTIAN, *brother to Viola.*
ANTONIO, *a sea captain, friend to Sebastian.*
A Sea Captain, *friend to Viola.*
VALENTINE,
CURIO, } *gentlemen attending on the Duke.*
SIR TOBY BELCH, *uncle (or perhaps cousin) to Olivia.*
SIR ANDREW AGUECHEEK.
MALVOLIO, *steward to Olivia.*
FABIAN,
FESTE, *a clown,* } *servants to Olivia.*

OLIVIA.
VIOLA.
MARIA, *Olivia's woman.*

Lords, Priests, Sailors, Officers, Musicians, and other
Attendants.

SCENE: *A city in Illyria, and the sea coast near it.*

ACT I

SCENE I

An apartment in the Duke's palace

Enter Duke, Curio, and other Lords; Musicians attending

Orsino. If music be the food of love, play on;
    Give me excess of it, that, surfeiting,
    The appetite may sicken, and so die.
    That strain again! it had a dying fall:
    O, it came o'er my ear like the sweet sound,
    That breathes upon a bank of violets,
    Stealing, and giving odour! Enough, no more,
    'Tis not so sweet now as it was before.
    O spirit of love, how quick and fresh art thou!
    That, notwithstanding thy capacity
    Receiveth as the sea, nought enters there,
    Of what validity and pitch soe'er,
    But falls into abatement and low price
    Even in a minute! so full of shapes is fancy,
    That it alone is high fantastical.
Curio. Will you go hunt, my lord?
Orsino.   What, Curio?
Curio. The hart.
Orsino. Why, so I do, the noblest that I have:
    O, when mine eyes did see Olivia first,
    Methought she purg'd the air of pestilence!
    That instant was I turn'd into a hart,

And my desires, like fell and cruel hounds,
E'er since pursue me.

Enter Valentine

How now, what news from her?

Valentine. So please my lord, I might not be admitted,
But from her handmaid do return this answer:
The element itself, till seven years' heat,
Shall not behold her face at ample view;
But, like a cloistress, she will veiled walk,
And water once a day her chamber round
With eye-offending brine: all this to season
A brother's dead love, which she would keep fresh
And lasting, in her sad remembrance.

Orsino. O, she that hath a heart of that fine frame
To pay this debt of love but to a brother,
How will she love, when the rich golden shaft
Hath kill'd the flock of all affections else
That live in her; when liver, brain, and heart,
These sovereign thrones, are all supplied and fill'd
Her sweet perfections with one self king!
Away before me, to sweet beds of flowers:
Love-thoughts lie rich, when canopied with bowers!   *Exeunt*

SCENE II

The sea-coast

Enter Viola, a Captain, and Sailors

Viola. What country, friends, is this?
Captain. This is Illyria, lady.
Viola. And what should I do in Illyria?
My brother he is in Elysium.
Perchance he is not drown'd: what think you,
   sailors?
Captain. It is perchance that you yourself were
   sav'd.
Viola. O my poor brother! and so perchance may he
   be.
Captain. True, madam, and, to comfort you with
   chance,
Assure yourself, after our ship did split,
When you, and those poor number saved with
   you,
Hung on our driving boat, I saw your brother,
Most provident in peril, bind himself,
(Courage and hope both teaching him the prac-
   tice)
To a strong mast, that liv'd upon the sea;
Where, like Arion on the dolphin's back,
I saw him hold acquaintance with the waves,
So long as I could see.

Viola. For saying so, there's gold:
    Mine own escape unfoldeth to my hope,
    Whereto thy speech serves for authority,
    The like of him. Know'st thou this country?
Captain. Ay, madam, well, for I was bred and born
    Not three hours' travel from this very place.
Viola. Who governs here?
Captain. A noble Duke, in nature as in name.
Viola. What is his name?
Captain. Orsino.
Viola. Orsino! I have heard my father name him:
    He was a bachelor then.
Captain. And so is now, or was so very late;
    For but a month ago I went from hence,
    And then 'twas fresh in murmur (as, you know,
    What great ones do the less will prattle of)
    That he did seek the love of fair Olivia.
Viola. What's she?
Captain. A virtuous maid, the daughter of a count
    That died some twelvemonth since, then leaving
        her
    In the protection of his son, her brother,
    Who shortly also died: for whose dear love
    (They say) she hath abjur'd the company
    And sight of men.
Viola.   O that I serv'd that lady,
    And might not be deliver'd to the world,—
    Till I had made mine own occasion mellow,—
    What my estate is!
Captain.   That were hard to compass;
    Because she will admit no kind of suit,
    No, not the Duke's.
Viola. There is a fair behaviour in thee, captain,
    And though that nature, with a beauteous wall,
    Doth oft close in pollution, yet of thee

I will believe thou hast a mind that suits
With this thy fair and outward character.
I prithee (and I'll pay thee bounteously)
Conceal me what I am, and be my aid
For such disguise as haply shall become
The form of my intent. I'll serve this Duke;
Thou shalt present me as an eunuch to him,
It may be worth thy pains; for I can sing,
And speak to him in many sorts of music,
That will allow me very worth his service.
What else may hap to time I will commit,
Only shape thou thy silence to my wit.

Captain. Be you his eunuch, and your mute I'll be;
When my tongue blabs, then let mine eyes not
see.

Viola. I thank thee: lead me on.   *Exeunt*

SCENE III

Olivia's house

Enter Sir Toby Belch and Maria

Sir Toby. What a plague means my niece, to take the death of her brother thus? I am sure care's an enemy to life.

Maria. By my troth, Sir Toby, you must come in earlier o' nights: your cousin, my lady, takes great exceptions to your ill hours.

Sir Toby. Why, let her except, before excepted.

Maria. Ay, but you must confine yourself within the modest limits of order.

Sir Toby. Confine? I'll confine myself no finer than I am: these clothes are good enough to drink in, and so be these boots too: an they be not, let them hang themselves in their own straps.

Maria. That quaffing and drinking will undo you: I heard my lady talk of it yesterday; and of a foolish knight that you brought in one night here to be her wooer.

Sir Toby. Who, Sir Andrew Aguecheek?

Maria. Ay, he.

Sir Toby. He's as tall a man as any 's in Illyria.

Maria. What's that to the purpose?

Sir Toby. Why, he has three thousand ducats a year.

Maria. Ay, but he'll have but a year in all these ducats: he's a very fool and a prodigal.

Sir Toby. Fie, that you'll say so! he plays o' the viol-de-gamboys, and speaks three or four languages word for word without book, and hath all the good gifts of nature.

Maria. He hath indeed, almost natural: for besides that he's a fool, he's a great quarreller; and but that he hath the gift of a coward, to allay the gust he hath in quarrelling, 'tis thought among the prudent he would quickly have the gift of a grave.

Sir Toby. By this hand, they are scoundrels and substractors that say so of him. Who are they?

Maria. They that add, moreover, he's drunk nightly in your company.

Sir Toby. With drinking healths to my niece: I'll drink to her as long as there is a passage in my throat and drink in Illyria: he's a coward and a coystrill that will not drink to my niece till his brains turn o' the toe, like a parish-top. What, wench? Castiliano vulgo; for here comes Sir Andrew Agueface.

Enter Sir Andrew Aguecheek

Sir Andrew. Sir Toby Belch! how now, Sir Toby Belch?

Sir Toby. Sweet Sir Andrew!

Sir Andrew. Bless you, fair shrew.

Maria. And you, too, sir.

Sir Toby. Accost, Sir Andrew, accost.

Sir Andrew. What's that?

Sir Toby. My niece's chambermaid.

Sir Andrew. Good Mistress Accost, I desire better acquaintance.

Maria. My name is Mary, sir.

Sir Andrew. Good Mistress Mary Accost,—

Sir Toby. You mistake, knight: 'accost' is front her, board her, woo her, assail her.

Sir Andrew. By my troth, I would not undertake her in this company. Is that the meaning of 'accost'?

Maria. Fare you well, gentlemen.

Sir Toby. An thou let part so, Sir Andrew, would thou mightst never draw sword again.

Sir Andrew. An you part so, mistress, I would I might never draw sword again. Fair lady, do you think you have fools in hand?

Maria. Sir, I have not you by the hand.

Sir Andrew. Marry, but you shall have, and here's my hand.

Maria. Now, sir, 'thought is free': I pray you, bring your hand to the buttery-bar, and let it drink.

Sir Andrew. Wherefore, sweet-heart? what's your metaphor?

Maria. It's dry, sir.

Sir Andrew. Why, I think so: I am not such an ass but I can keep my hand dry. But what's your jest?

Maria. A dry jest, sir.

Sir Andrew. Are you full of them?

Maria. Ay, sir, I have them at my fingers' ends: marry, now I let go your hand, I am barren.   *Exit*

Sir Toby. O knight, thou lack'st a cup of canary: when did I see thee so put down?

Sir Andrew. Never in your life, I think, unless you see canary put me down. Methinks sometimes I have no more wit than a Christian or an ordinary man has: but I am a great eater of beef, and I believe that does harm to my wit.

Sir Toby. No question.

Sir Andrew. An I thought that, I 'ld forswear it. I'll ride home to-morrow, Sir Toby.

Sir Toby. Pourquoi, my dear knight?

Sir Andrew. What is 'pourquoi'? do or not do? I
would I had bestowed that time in the tongues
that I have in fencing, dancing and bear-baiting:
O, had I but followed the arts!

Sir Toby. Then had'st thou had an excellent head of
hair.

Sir Andrew. Why, would that have mended my
hair?

Sir Toby. Past question; for thou seest it will not curl
by nature.

Sir Andrew. But it becomes me well enough, does 't
not?

Sir Toby. Excellent, it hangs like flax on a distaff;
and I hope to see a housewife take thee between
her legs and spin it off.

Sir Andrew. Faith, I'll home to-morrow, Sir Toby:
your niece will not be seen, or if she be, it's four
to one she'll none of me: the count himself here
hard by woos her.

Sir Toby. She'll none o' the count, she'll not match
above her degree, neither in estate, years, nor wit;
I have heard her swear 't. Tut, there's life in 't,
man.

Sir Andrew. I'll stay a month longer. I am a fellow
o' the strangest mind i' the world; I delight in
masques and revels sometimes altogether.

Sir Toby. Art thou good at these kickshawses,
knight?

Sir Andrew. As any man in Illyria, whatsoever he
be, under the degree of my betters, and yet I will
not compare with an old man.

Sir Toby. What is thy excellence in a galliard,
knight?

Sir Andrew. Faith, I can cut a caper.

Sir Toby. And I can cut the mutton to 't.

Sir Andrew. And I think I have the back-trick, simply as strong as any man in Illyria.

Sir Toby. Wherefore are these things hid? wherefore have these gifts a curtain before 'em? are they like to take dust, like Mrs. Mall's picture? why dost thou not go to church in a galliard, and come home in a coranto? My very walk should be a jig; I would not so much as make water but in a sink-a-pace. What dost thou mean? Is it a world to hide virtues in? I did think, by the excellent constitution of thy leg, it was form'd under the star of a galliard.

Sir Andrew. Ay, 'tis strong, and it does indifferent well in a flame-colour'd stock. Shall we set about some revels?

Sir Toby. What shall we do else? were we not born under Taurus?

Sir Andrew. Taurus? That's sides and heart.

Sir Toby. No, sir, it is legs and thighs. Let me see thee caper: ha! higher: ha, ha! excellent!

Exeunt

SCENE IV

The Duke's palace

Enter Valentine, and Viola in man's attire

Valentine. If the Duke continue these favours towards you, Cesario, you are like to be much advanc'd: he hath known you but three days, and already you are no stranger.

Viola. You either fear his humour or my negligence, that you call in question the continuance of his love: is he inconstant, sir, in his favours?

Valentine. No, believe me.

Viola. I thank you. Here comes the count.

Enter Duke, Curio, and Attendants

Orsino. Who saw Cesario, ho?

Viola. On your attendance, my lord; here.

Orsino. Stand you a while aloof. Cesario,
Thou know'st no less but all; I have unclasp'd
To thee the book even of my secret soul:
Therefore, good youth, address thy gait unto her,
Be not denied access, stand at her doors,
And tell them, there thy fixed foot shall grow
Till thou have audience.

Viola. Sure, my noble lord,
If she be so abandon'd to her sorrow
As it is spoke, she never will admit me.

Orsino. Be clamorous, and leap all civil bounds
Rather than make unprofited return.
Viola. Say I do speak with her, my lord, what then?
Orsino. O then, unfold the passion of my love,
Surprise her with discourse of my dear faith:
It shall become thee well to act my woes;
She will attend it better in thy youth
Than in a nuncio's of more grave aspect.
Viola. I think not so, my lord.
Orsino.   Dear lad, believe it;
For they shall yet belie thy happy years,
That say thou art a man: Diana's lip
Is not more smooth, and rubious; thy small pipe
Is as the maiden's organ, shrill, and sound,
And all is semblative a woman's part.
I know thy constellation is right apt
For this affair: some four or five attend him,
All, if you will; for I myself am best
When least in company. Prosper well in this,
And thou shalt live as freely as thy lord,
To call his fortunes thine.
Viola.   I'll do my best
To woo your lady: (*aside*) yet a barful strife!
Whoe'er I woo, myself would be his wife.
                                        Exeunt

SCENE V

Olivia's house

Enter Maria and Clown

Maria. Nay, either tell me where thou hast been, or I will not open my lips so wide as a bristle may enter, in way of thy excuse: my lady will hang thee for thy absence.

Feste. Let her hang me: he that is well hang'd in this world needs to fear no colours.

Maria. Make that good.

Feste. He shall see none to fear.

Maria. A good lenten answer: I can tell thee where that saying was born, of 'I fear no colours.'

Feste. Where, good Mistress Mary?

Maria. In the wars, and that may you be bold to say in your foolery.

Feste. Well, God give them wisdom that have it; and those that are fools, let them use their talents.

Maria. Yet you will be hang'd for being so long absent, or, to be turn'd away, is not that as good as a hanging to you?

Feste. Many a good hanging prevents a bad marriage; and, for turning away, let summer bear it out.

Maria. You are resolute, then?

Feste. Not so, neither; but I am resolv'd on two points.

Maria. That if one break, the other will hold; or, if both break, your gaskins fall.

Feste. Apt, in good faith, very apt. Well go thy way; if Sir Toby would leave drinking, thou wert as witty a piece of Eve's flesh as any in Illyria.

Maria. Peace, you rogue, no more o' that. Here

comes my lady: make your excuse wisely, you
were best.   *Exit*
Feste. Wit, an 't be thy will, put me into good fooling! Those wits that think they have thee, do very
oft prove fools; and I, that am sure I lack thee,
may pass for a wise man: for what says Quina-
palus? 'Better a witty fool than a foolish wit.'

Enter Lady Olivia with Malvolio

God bless thee, lady!
Olivia. Take the fool away.
Feste. Do you not hear, fellows? Take away the
lady.
Olivia. Go to, you're a dry fool; I'll no more of you:
besides, you grow dishonest.
Feste. Two faults, madonna, that drink and good
counsel will amend: for give the dry fool drink,
then is the fool not dry: bid the dishonest man
mend himself; if he mend, he is no longer dishonest; if he cannot, let the botcher mend him. Any
thing that's mended is but patch'd: virtue that
transgresses is but patch'd with sin, and sin that
amends is but patched with virtue. If that this
simple syllogism will serve, so; if it will not, what
remedy? As there is no true cuckold but calamity,
so beauty's a flower. The lady bade take away
the fool, therefore I say again, take her away.
Olivia. Sir, I bade them take away you.
Feste. Misprision in the highest degree! Lady,
cucullus non facit monachum; that's as much to
say as I wear not motley in my brain. Good madonna, give me leave to prove you a fool.
Olivia. Can you do it?
Feste. Dexteriously, good madonna.

Olivia. Make your proof.

Feste. I must catechize you for it, madonna: good my mouse of virtue, answer me.

Olivia. Well, sir, for want of other idleness, I'll bide your proof.

Feste. Good madonna, why mournest thou?

Olivia. Good fool, for my brother's death.

Feste. I think his soul is in hell, madonna.

Olivia. I know his soul is in heaven, fool.

Feste. The more fool, madonna, to mourn for your brother's soul being in heaven. Take away the fool, gentlemen.

Olivia. What think you of this fool, Malvolio? doth he not mend?

Malvolio. Yes, and shall do till the pangs of death shake him: infirmity, that decays the wise, doth ever make the better fool.

Feste. God send you, sir, a speedy infirmity, for the better increasing your folly! Sir Toby will be sworn that I am no fox, but he will not pass his word for two pence that you are no fool.

Olivia. How say you to that, Malvolio?

Malvolio. I marvel your ladyship takes delight in such a barren rascal: I saw him put down the other day with an ordinary fool, that has no more brain than a stone. Look you now, he's out of his guard already; unless you laugh and minister occasion to him, he is gagg'd. I protest, I take these wise men, that crow so at these set kind of fools, no better than the fools' zanies.

Olivia. O, you are sick of self-love, Malvolio, and taste with a distemper'd appetite. To be generous, guiltless and of free disposition, is to take those things for bird-bolts that you deem cannon-bullets: there is no slander in an allow'd fool, though he do nothing but rail; nor no railing in a known discreet man, though he do nothing but reprove.

Feste. Now Mercury endue thee with leasing, for thou speak'st well of fools!

Re-enter Maria

Maria. Madam, there is at the gate a young gentleman much desires to speak with you.

Olivia. From the Count Orsino, is it?

Maria. I know not, madam, 'tis a fair young man, and well attended.

Olivia. Who of my people hold him in delay?

Maria. Sir Toby, madam, your kinsman.

Olivia. Fetch him off, I pray you, he speaks nothing but madman: fie on him! (*exit Maria.*) Go you, Malvolio: if it be a suit from the count, I am sick, or not at home; what you will, to dismiss it. (*exit Malvolio.*) Now you see, sir, how your fooling grows old, and people dislike it.

Feste. Thou hast spoke for us, madonna, as if thy eldest son should be a fool; whose skull Jove cram with brains! for,—here he comes,—one of thy kin has a most weak pia mater.

Enter Sir Toby

Olivia. By mine honour, half drunk. What is he at the gate, cousin?

Sir Toby. A gentleman.

Olivia. A gentleman? what gentleman?

Sir Toby. 'Tis a gentleman here—a plague o' these pickled herring! How now, sot?

Feste. Good Sir Toby!

Olivia. Cousin, cousin, how have you come so early by this lethargy?

Sir Toby. Lechery! I defy lechery. There's one at the
  gate.

Olivia. Ay, marry, what is he?

Sir Toby. Let him be the devil, an he will, I care not:
  give me faith, say I. Well, it's all one.   *Exit*

Olivia. What's a drunken man like, fool?

Feste. Like a drown'd man, a fool, and a mad man:
  one draught above heat makes him a fool, the sec-
  ond mads him, and a third drowns him.

Olivia. Go thou and seek the crowner, and let him
  sit o' my coz; for he's in the third degree of drink;
  he's drown'd: go look after him.

Feste. He is but mad yet, madonna, and the fool
  shall look to the madman.   *Exit*

Re-enter Malvolio

Malvolio. Madam, yond young fellow swears he will
  speak with you. I told him you were sick; he takes
  on him to understand so much, and therefore
  comes to speak with you. I told him you were
  asleep; he seems to have a foreknowledge of that
  too, and therefore comes to speak with you. What
  is to be said to him, lady? he's fortified against
  any denial.

Olivia. Tell him, he shall not speak with me.

Malvolio. Has been told so; and he says, he'll stand
  at your door like a sheriff's post, and be the sup-
  porter to a bench, but he'll speak with you.

Olivia. What kind o' man is he?

Malvolio. Why, of mankind.

Olivia. What manner of man?

Malvolio. Of very ill manner: he'll speak with you,
  will you or no.

Olivia. Of what personage and years is he?

Malvolio. Not yet old enough for a man, nor young

enough for a boy; as a squash is before 'tis a
peascod, or a codling when 'tis almost an apple:
'tis with him in standing water, between boy and
man. He is very well-favour'd and he speaks very
shrewishly; one would think his mother's milk
were scarce out of him.

Olivia. Let him approach: call in my gentlewoman.

Malvolio. Gentlewoman, my lady calls. *Exit*

Re-enter Maria

Olivia. Give me my veil: come, throw it o'er my
face;
We'll once more hear Orsino's embassy.

Enter Viola, and Attendants

Viola. The honourable lady of the house, which is
she?

Olivia. Speak to me, I shall answer for her. Your
will?

Viola. Most radiant, exquisite and unmatchable
beauty,—I pray you, tell me if this be the lady of
the house, for I never saw her: I would be loath to
cast away my speech; for besides that it is excellently well penn'd, I have taken great pain to con
it. Good beauties, let me sustain no scorn; I am
very comptible, even to the least sinister usage.

Olivia. Whence came you, sir?

Viola. I can say little more than I have studied, and
that question's out of my part. Good gentle one,
give me modest assurance if you be the lady of
the house, that I may proceed in my speech.

Olivia. Are you a comedian?

Viola. No, my profound heart: and yet, by the very
fangs of malice I swear, I am not that I play. Are
you the lady of the house?

Olivia. If I do not usurp myself, I am.

Viola. Most certain, if you are she, you do usurp yourself; for what is yours to bestow is not yours to reserve. But this is from my commission: I will on with my speech in your praise, and then show you the heart of my message.

Olivia. Come to what is important in 't: I forgive you the praise.

Viola. Alas, I took great pains to study it, and 'tis poetical.

Olivia. It is the more like to be feigned. I pray you, keep it in. I heard you were saucy at my gates, and allow'd your approach rather to wonder at you than to hear you. If you be not mad, be gone; if you have reason, be brief: 'tis not that time of moon with me to make one in so skipping a dialogue.

Maria. Will you hoist sail, sir? here lies your way.

Viola. No, good swabber, I am to hull here a little longer. Some mollification for your giant, sweet lady.

Olivia. Tell me your mind.

Viola. I am a messenger.

Olivia. Sure, you have some hideous matter to deliver, when the courtesy of it is so fearful. Speak your office.

Viola. It alone concerns your ear. I bring no overture of war, no taxation of homage: I hold the olive in my hand; my words are as full of peace as matter.

Olivia. Yet you began rudely. What are you? what would you?

Viola. The rudeness that hath appear'd in me have I learn'd from my entertainment. What I am, and what I would, are as secret as maidenhead; to your ears, divinity; to any other's, profanation.

Olivia. Give us the place alone, we will hear this divinity. (*exeunt Maria and Attendants.*) Now, sir, what is your text?

Viola. Most sweet lady.

Olivia. A comfortable doctrine, and much may be said of it. Where lies your text?

Viola. In Orsino's bosom.

Olivia. In his bosom? In what chapter of his bosom?

Viola. To answer by the method, in the first of his heart.

Olivia. O, I have read it: it is heresy. Have you no more to say?

Viola. Good madam, let me see your face.

Olivia. Have you any commission from your lord to negotiate with my face? You are now out of your text: but we will draw the curtain and show you the picture. Look you, sir, such a one I was this present: is 't not well done?   *Unveiling*

Viola. Excellently done, if God did all.

Olivia. 'Tis in grain, sir, 'twill endure wind and weather.

Viola. 'Tis beauty truly blent, whose red and white Nature's own sweet and cunning hand laid on:
Lady, you are the cruell'st she alive,
If you will lead these graces to the grave,
And leave the world no copy.

Olivia. O, sir, I will not be so hard-hearted; I will give out divers schedules of my beauty: it shall be inventoried, and every particle and utensil labelled to my will: as, item, two lips, indifferent red; item, two grey eyes, with lids to them; item, one neck, one chin, and so forth. Were you sent hither to praise me?

Viola. I see you what you are, you are too proud;
But, if you were the devil, you are fair.

My lord and master loves you: O, such love
Could be but recompens'd, though you were
   crown'd
The nonpareil of beauty!

Olivia.   How does he love me?

Viola. With adorations, fertile tears,
With groans that thunder love, with sighs of fire.

Olivia. Your lord does know my mind; I cannot love
   him:
Yet I suppose him virtuous, know him noble,
Of great estate, of fresh and stainless youth;
In voices well divulg'd, free, learn'd and valiant;
And in dimension, and the shape of nature,
A gracious person: but yet I cannot love him;
He might have took his answer long ago.

Viola. If I did love you in my master's flame,
With such a suffering, such a deadly life,
In your denial I would find no sense;
I would not understand it.

Olivia.   Why, what would you?

Viola. Make me a willow cabin at your gate,
And call upon my soul within the house;
Write loyal cantons of contemned love
And sing them loud even in the dead of night;
Halloo your name to the reverberate hills,
And make the babbling gossip of the air
Cry out 'Olivia!' O, you should not rest
Between the elements of air and earth,
But you should pity me!

Olivia.   You might do much.
What is your parentage?

Viola. Above my fortunes, yet my state is well:
I am a gentleman.

Olivia.   Get you to your lord;
I cannot love him: let him send no more,
Unless, perchance, you come to me again,

To tell me how he takes it. Fare you well:
I thank you for your pains: spend this for me.
Viola. I am no fee'd post, lady; keep your purse:
My master, not myself, lacks recompense.
Love make his heart of flint, that you shall love,
And let your fervour like my master's be,
Plac'd in contempt! Farewell, fair cruelty.   *Exit*
Olivia. 'What is your parentage?'
'Above my fortunes, yet my state is well:
I am a gentleman.' I'll be sworn thou art;
Thy tongue, thy face, thy limbs, actions, and
    spirit,
Do give thee five-fold blazon: not too fast: soft,
    soft!
Unless the master were the man. How now?
Even so quickly may one catch the plague?
Methinks I feel this youth's perfections
With an invisible and subtle stealth
To creep in at mine eyes. Well, let it be.
What ho, Malvolio!

Re-enter Malvolio

Malvolio.   Here, madam, at your service.
Olivia. Run after that same peevish messenger,
The county's man: he left this ring behind him,
Would I or not: tell him I'll none of it.
Desire him not to flatter with his lord,
Nor hold him up with hopes; I am not for him:
If that the youth will come this way to-morrow,
I'll give him reasons for 't: hie thee, Malvolio.
Malvolio. Madam, I will.   *Exit*
Olivia. I do I know not what, and fear to find
Mine eye too great a flatterer for my mind.
Fate, show thy force: ourselves we do not owe;
What is decreed, must be; and be this so.   *Exit*

ACT II

SCENE I

The sea-coast

Enter Antonio and Sebastian

Antonio. Will you stay no longer? nor will you not
that I go with you?

Sebastian. By your patience, no. My stars shine
darkly over me: the malignancy of my fate might
perhaps distemper yours; therefore I shall crave
of you your leave, that I may bear my evils
alone: it were a bad recompense for your love, to
lay any of them on you.

Antonio. Let me yet know of you whither you are
bound.

Sebastian. No, sooth, sir: my determinate voyage is
mere extravagancy. But I perceive in you so excellent a touch of modesty, that you will not
extort from me what I am willing to keep in;
therefore it charges me in manners the rather to
express myself. You must know of me then, Antonio, my name is Sebastian, which I call'd Ro-
derigo; my father was that Sebastian of Messaline,
whom I know you have heard of. He left behind
him myself and a sister, both born in an hour: if
the heavens had been pleas'd, would we had so
ended! but you, sir, altered that; for some hour

before you took me from the breach of the sea was my sister drown'd.

Antonio. Alas the day!

Sebastian. A lady, sir, though it was said she much resembled me, was yet of many accounted beautiful: but, though I could not with such estimable wonder overfar believe that, yet thus far I will boldly publish her: she bore a mind that envy could not but call fair. She is drown'd already, sir, with salt water, though I seem to drown her remembrance again with more.

Antonio. Pardon me, sir, your bad entertainment.

Sebastian. O good Antonio, forgive me your trouble.

Antonio. If you will not murder me for my love, let me be your servant.

Sebastian. If you will not undo what you have done, that is, kill him whom you have recover'd, desire it not. Fare ye well at once: my bosom is full of kindness, and I am yet so near the manners of my mother, that upon the least occasion more mine eyes will tell tales of me. I am bound to the Count Orsino's court: farewell.   *Exit*

Antonio. The gentleness of all the gods go with thee!
I have many enemies in Orsino's court,
Else would I very shortly see thee there.
But, come what may, I do adore thee so,
That danger shall seem sport, and I will go.
                                              Exit

SCENE II

A street

Enter Viola, Malvolio following

Malvolio. Were not you e'en now with the Countess
Olivia?

Viola. Even now, sir; on a moderate pace I have
since arriv'd but hither.

Malvolio. She returns this ring to you, sir: you might
have saved me my pains, to have taken it away
yourself. She adds moreover, that you should put
your lord into a desperate assurance she will none
of him: and one thing more, that you be never so
hardy to come again in his affairs, unless it be to
report your lord's taking of this. Receive it so.

Viola. She took the ring of me: I'll none of it.

Malvolio. Come, sir, you peevishly threw it to her;
and her will is, it should be so return'd: if it be
worth stooping for, there it lies, in your eye; if
not, be it his that finds it.   *Exit*

Viola. I left no ring with her: what means this lady?
Fortune forbid my outside have not charm'd her!
She made good view of me, indeed, so much,
That methought her eyes had lost her tongue,
For she did speak in starts distractedly.
She loves me, sure; the cunning of her passion

Invites me in this churlish messenger.
None of my lord's ring? why, he sent her none.
I am the man: if it be so, as 'tis,
Poor lady, she were better love a dream.
Disguise, I see thou art a wickedness,
Wherein the pregnant enemy does much.
How easy is it for the proper-false
In women's waxen hearts to set their forms!
Alas, our frailty is the cause, not we!
For such as we are made of, such we be.
How will this fadge? my master loves her dearly;
And I, poor monster, fond as much on him;
And she, mistaken, seems to dote on me.
What will become of this? As I am man,
My state is desperate for my master's love;
As I am woman,—now alas the day!—
What thriftless sighs shall poor Olivia breathe!
O time! thou must untangle this, not I;
It is too hard a knot for me to untie!   *Exit*

SCENE III

Olivia's house

Enter Sir Toby and Sir Andrew

Sir Toby. Approach, Sir Andrew: not to be a-bed after midnight is to be up betimes; and 'diluculo surgere,' thou know'st,—

Sir Andrew. Nay, by my troth, I know not: but I know, to be up late is to be up late.

Sir Toby. A false conclusion: I hate it as an unfill'd can. To be up after midnight and to go to bed then, is early: so that to go to bed after midnight is to go to bed betimes. Does not our life consist of the four elements?

Sir Andrew. Faith, so they say; but I think it rather consists of eating and drinking.

Sir Toby. Thou 'rt a scholar; let us therefore eat and drink. Marian, I say! a stoup of wine!

Enter Clown

Sir Andrew. Here comes the fool, i' faith.

Feste. How now, my hearts! did you never see the picture of 'we three'?

Sir Toby. Welcome, ass. Now let's have a catch.

Sir Andrew. By my troth, the fool has an excellent breast. I had rather than forty shillings I had such a leg, and so sweet a breath to sing, as the fool has. In sooth, thou wast in very gracious fooling last night, when thou spokest of Pigrogromitus, of the Vapians passing the equinoctial of Queubus:

'twas very good, i' faith. I sent thee sixpence for
thy leman: hadst it?

Feste. I did impetticoat thy gratillity; for Malvolio's
nose is no whipstock: my lady has a white hand,
and the Mermidons are no bottle-ale houses.

Sir Andrew. Excellent! why, this is the best fooling,
when all is done. Now, a song.

Sir Toby. Come on, there is sixpence for you: let's
have a song.

Sir Andrew. There's a testril of me too: if one knight
give a—

Feste. Would you have a love-song, or a song of
good life?

Sir Toby. A love-song, a love-song.

Sir Andrew. Ay, ay: I care not for good life.

Feste. (sings)

    O mistress mine, where are you roaming?
    O, stay and hear; your true love's coming,
        That can sing both high and low:
    Trip no further, pretty sweeting;
    Journeys end in lovers meeting,
        Every wise man's son doth know.

Sir Andrew. Excellent good, i' faith.

Sir Toby. Good, good.

Feste. (sings)

    What is love? 'tis not hereafter;
    Present mirth hath present laughter;
        What's to come is still unsure:
    In delay there lies no plenty;
    Then come kiss me, sweet and twenty,
        Youth's a stuff will not endure.

Sir Andrew. A mellifluous voice, as I am true knight.

Sir Toby. A contagious breath.

Sir Andrew. Very sweet and contagious, i' faith.

Sir Toby. To hear by the nose, it is dulcet in con-

tagion. But shall we make the welkin dance indeed? shall we rouse the night-owl in a catch that will draw three souls out of one weaver? shall we do that?

Sir Andrew. An you love me, let's do 't: I am dog at a catch.

Feste. By 'r lady, sir, and some dogs will catch well.

Sir Andrew. Most certain. Let our catch be, 'Thou knave.'

Feste. 'Hold thy peace, thou knave,' knight? I shall be constrained in 't to call thee knave, knight.

Sir Andrew. 'Tis not the first time I have constrained one to call me knave. Begin, fool: it begins 'Hold thy peace.'

Feste. I shall never begin if I hold my peace.

Sir Andrew. Good, i' faith. Come, begin.

Catch sung

Enter Maria

Maria. What a caterwauling do you keep here! If my lady have not call'd up her steward Malvolio and bid him turn you out of doors, never trust me.

Sir Toby. My lady's a Cataian, we are politicians, Malvolio's a Peg-a-Ramsey, and 'Three merry men be we.' Am not I consanguineous? am I not of her blood? Tillyvally. Lady! (*sings*) 'There dwelt a man in Babylon, lady, lady!'

Feste. Beshrew me, the knight's in admirable fooling.

Sir Andrew. Ay, he does well enough if he be dispos'd, and so do I too: he does it with a better grace, but I do it more natural.

Sir Toby. (*sings*) 'O, the twelfth day of December',—

Maria. For the love o' God, peace!

Enter Malvolio

Malvolio. My masters, are you mad? or what are you? Have you no wit, manners, nor honesty, but to gabble like tinkers at this time of night? Do ye make an alehouse of my lady's house, that ye squeak out your coziers' catches without any mitigation or remorse of voice? Is there no respect of place, persons, nor time in you?

Sir Toby. We did keep time, sir, in our catches. Sneck up!

Malvolio. Sir Toby, I must be round with you. My lady bade me tell you, that, though she harbours you as her kinsman, she's nothing allied to your disorders. If you can separate yourself and your misdemeanours, you are welcome to the house; if not, an it would please you to take leave of her, she is very willing to bid you farewell.

Sir Toby. 'Farewell, dear heart, since I must needs be gone.'

Maria. Nay, good Sir Toby.

Feste. 'His eyes do show his days are almost done.'

Malvolio. Is 't even so?

Sir Toby. 'But I will never die.'

Feste. Sir Toby, there you lie.

Malvolio. This is much credit to you.

Sir Toby. 'Shall I bid him go?'

Feste. 'What an if you do?'

Sir Toby. 'Shall I bid him go, and spare not?'

Feste. 'O no, no, no, no, you dare not.'

Sir Toby. Out o' tune, sir: ye lie. (*to Malvolio*) Art any more than a steward? Dost thou think, because thou art virtuous, there shall be no more cakes and ale?

Feste. Yes, by Saint Anne, and ginger shall be hot i' the mouth too.

Sir Toby. Thou 'rt i' the right. Go, Sir, rub your chain with crumbs. A stoup of wine, Maria!

Malvolio. Mistress Mary, if you priz'd my lady's favour at any thing more than contempt, you would not give means for this uncivil rule: she shall know of it, by this hand.   *Exit*

Maria. Go shake your ears.

Sir Andrew. 'Twere as good a deed as to drink when a man's a-hungry, to challenge him the field, and then to break promise with him, and make a fool of him.

Sir Toby. Do 't knight: I'll write thee a challenge; or I'll deliver thy indignation to him by word of mouth.

Maria. Sweet Sir Toby, be patient for to-night: since the youth of the count's was to-day with my lady, she is much out of quiet. For Monsieur Malvolio, let me alone with him: if I do not gull him into an ayword, and make him a common recreation, do not think I have wit enough to lie straight in my bed: I know I can do it.

Sir Toby. Possess us, possess us; tell us something of of him.

Maria. Marry, sir, sometimes he is a kind of puritan.

Sir Andrew. O, if I thought that, I 'ld beat him like a dog!

Sir Toby. What, for being a puritan? thy exquisite reason, dear knight?

Sir Andrew. I have no exquisite reason for 't, but I have reason good enough.

Maria. The devil a puritan that he is, or anything constantly but a time-pleaser, an affection'd ass, that cons state without book, and utters it by great swarths: the best persuaded of himself, so cramm'd, as he thinks, with excellencies, that it is his grounds of faith that all that look on him love him; and on that vice in him will my revenge find notable cause to work.

Sir Toby. What wilt thou do?

Maria. I will drop in his way some obscure epistles of love, wherein, by the colour of his beard, the shape of his leg, the manner of his gait, the expressure of his eye, forehead, and complexion, he shall find himself most feelingly personated. I can write very like my lady your niece; on a forgotten matter we can hardly make distinction of our hands.

Sir Toby. Excellent! I smell a device.

Sir Andrew. I have 't in my nose too.

Sir Toby. He shall think, by the letters that thou wilt drop, that they come from my niece, and that she's in love with him.

Maria. My purpose is, indeed, a horse of that colour.

Sir Andrew. And your horse now would make him an ass.

Maria. Ass, I doubt not.

Sir Andrew. O, 'twill be admirable!

Maria. Sport royal, I warrant you: I know my physic will work with him. I will plant you two, and let the fool make a third, where he shall find the letter: observe his construction of it. For this night, to bed, and dream on the event. Farewell.   *Exit*

Sir Toby. Good night, Penthesilea.

Sir Andrew. Before me, she's a good wench.

Sir Toby. She's a beagle, true-bred, and one that adores me: what o' that?

Sir Andrew. I was ador'd once too.

Sir Toby. Let's to bed, knight. Thou hadst need send for more money.

Sir Andrew. If I cannot recover your niece, I am a foul way out.

Sir Toby. Send for money, knight; if thou hast her not i' the end, call me cut.

Sir Andrew. If I do not, never trust me, take it how you will.

Sir Toby. Come, come, I'll go burn some sack; 'tis too late to go to bed now; come, knight; come, knight.   *Exeunt*

SCENE IV

The Duke's palace

Enter Duke, Viola, Curio, and others

Orsino. Give me some music. Now, good morrow,
   friends.
   Now, good Cesario, but that piece of song,
   That old and antique song we heard last night:
   Methought it did relieve my passion much,
   More than light airs, and recollected terms
   Of these most brisk and giddy-paced times:
   Come, but one verse.
Curio. He is not here, so please your lordship, that
   should sing it.
Orsino. Who was it?
Curio. Feste, the jester, my lord; a fool that the lady
   Olivia's father took much delight in. He is about
   the house.
Orsino. Seek him out, and play the tune the while.
                              Exit Curio. Music plays
   Come hither, boy: if ever thou shalt love,
   In the sweet pangs of it remember me;
   For such as I am all true lovers are,
   Unstaid and skittish in all motions else,
   Save in the constant image of the creature
   That is belov'd. How dost thou like this tune?

Viola. It gives a very echo to the seat
   Where love is thron'd.
Orsino.   Thou dost speak masterly:
   My life upon 't, young though thou art, thine eye
   Hath stay'd upon some favour that it loves:
   Hath it not, boy?
Viola.   A little, by your favour.
Orsino. What kind of woman is 't?
Viola.   Of your complexion.
Orsino. She is not worth thee, then. What years, i'
      faith?
Viola. About your years, my lord.
Orsino. Too old, by heaven: let still the woman take
   An elder than herself; so wears she to him,
   So sways she level in her husband's heart:
   For, boy, however we do praise ourselves,
   Our fancies are more giddy and unfirm,
   More longing, wavering, sooner lost and won,
   Than women's are.
Viola.   I think it well, my lord.
Orsino. Then let thy love be younger than thyself,
   Or thy affection cannot hold the bent;
   For women are as roses, whose fair flower
   Being once display'd, doth fall that very hour.
Viola. And so they are: alas, that they are so;
   To die, even when they to perfection grow!

               Re-enter Curio and Clown

Orsino. O, fellow, come, the song we had last night.
   Mark it, Cesario, it is old and plain;
   The spinsters and the knitters in the sun,
   And the free maids that weave their thread with
      bones,
   Do use to chant it: it is silly sooth,
   And dallies with the innocence of love,
   Like the old age.

Feste. Are you ready, sir?
Orsino. Ay; prithee sing.   *Music*

SONG

Feste. Come away, come away, death,
    And in sad cypress let me be laid;
Fly away, fly away, breath;
    I am slain by a fair cruel maid.
My shroud of white, stuck all with yew,
        O, prepare it!
My part of death, no one so true
        Did share it.

Not a flower, not a flower sweet,
    On my black coffin let there be strown;
Not a friend, not a friend greet
    My poor corpse, where my bones shall
        be thrown:
A thousand thousand sighs to save,
        Lay me, O, where
Sad true lover never find my grave,
        To weep there!

Orsino. There's for thy pains.
Feste. No pains, sir, I take pleasure in singing, sir.
Orsino. I'll pay thy pleasure then.
Feste. Truly, sir, and pleasure will be paid, one time
    or another.
Orsino. Give me now leave to leave thee.
Feste. Now, the melancholy god protect thee, and
    the tailor make thy doublet of changeable taffeta,
    for thy mind is a very opal. I would have men of
    such constancy put to sea, that their business
    might be every thing, and their intent every
    where; for that's it that always makes a good
    voyage of nothing. Farewell.   *Exit*

Orsino. Let all the rest give place.
                              Curio and Attendants retire
                                        Once more, Cesario,
   Get thee to yond same sovereign cruelty:
   Tell her my love, more noble than the world,
   Prizes not quantity of dirty lands;
   The parts that fortune hath bestow'd upon her,
   Tell her, I hold as giddily as fortune;
   But 'tis that miracle, and queen of gems
   That nature pranks her in, attracts my soul.
Viola. But if she cannot love you, sir?
Orsino. I cannot be so answer'd.
Viola.   Sooth, but you must.
   Say that some lady, as perhaps there is,
   Hath for your love as great a pang of heart
   As you have for Olivia: you cannot love her;
   You tell her so; must she not then be answer'd?
Orsino. There is no woman's sides
   Can bide the beating of so strong a passion
   As love doth give my heart; no woman's heart
   So big, to hold so much; they lack retention.
   Alas, their love may be call'd appetite,—
   No motion of the liver, but the palate,—
   That suffer surfeit, cloyment and revolt;
   But mine is all as hungry as the sea,
   And can digest as much: make no compare
   Between that love a woman can bear me
   And that I owe Olivia.
Viola.   Ay, but I know,—
Orsino. What dost thou know?
Viola. Too well what love women to men may owe:
   In faith, they are as true of heart as we.
   My father had a daughter lov'd a man,
   As it might be, perhaps, were I a woman,
   I should your lordship.

Orsino. And what's her history?
Viola. A blank, my lord. She never told her love,
    But let concealment, like a worm i' the bud,
    Feed on her damask cheek: she pin'd in thought
    And with a green and yellow melancholy
    She sat like patience on a monument,
    Smiling at grief. Was not this love indeed?
    We men may say more, swear more, but indeed
    Our shows are more than will; for still we prove
    Much in our vows, but little in our love.
Orsino. But died thy sister of her love, my boy?
Viola. I am all the daughters of my father's house,
    And all the brothers too: and yet I know not.
    Sir, shall I to this lady?
Orsino. Ay that's the theme.
    To her in haste; give her this jewel; say,
    My love can give no place, bide no denay.

                               Exeunt

SCENE V

Olivia's garden

Enter Sir Toby, Sir Andrew, and Fabian

Sir Toby. Come thy ways, Signior Fabian.

Fabian. Nay, I'll come: if I lose a scruple of this sport, let me be boil'd to death with melancholy.

Sir Toby. Wouldst thou not be glad to have the niggardly rascally sheep-biter come by some notable shame?

Fabian. I would exult, man: you know, he brought me out o' favour with my lady about a bear-baiting here.

Sir Toby. To anger him we'll have the bear again, and we will fool him black and blue, shall we not, Sir Andrew?

Sir Andrew. An we do not, it is pity of our lives.

Sir Toby. Here comes the little villain.

Enter Maria

How now, my metal of India?

Maria. Get ye all three into the box-tree: Malvolio's coming down this walk: he has been yonder i' the sun practising behaviour to his own shadow this half hour: observe him, for the love of mockery; for I know this letter will make a contemplative idiot of him. Close, in the name of jesting! Lie

thou there (*throws down a letter*); for here comes the trout that must be caught with tickling. *Exit*

Enter Malvolio

Malvolio. 'Tis but fortune, all is fortune. Maria once told me she did affect me, and I have heard herself come thus near, that, should she fancy, it should be one of my complexion. Besides, she uses me with a more exalted respect than any one else that follows her. What should I think on 't?

Sir Toby. Here's an overweening rogue!

Fabian. O, peace! Contemplation makes a rare turkey-cock of him: how he jets under his advanc'd plumes!

Sir Andrew. 'Slight, I could so beat the rogue!

Fabian. Peace, I say.

Malvolio. To be Count Malvolio!

Sir Toby. Ah, rogue!

Sir Andrew. Pistol him, pistol him.

Fabian. Peace, peace!

Malvolio. There is example for 't; the lady of the Strachy married the yeoman of the wardrobe.

Sir Andrew. Fie on him Jezebel!

Fabian. O, peace! now he's deeply in: look how imagination blows him.

Malvolio. Having been three months married to her, sitting in my state,—

Sir Toby. O, for a stone-bow, to hit him in the eye!

Malvolio. Calling my officers about me, in my branch'd velvet gown; having come from a day-bed, where I have left Olivia sleeping,—

Sir Toby. Fire and brimstone!

Fabian. O, peace, peace!

Malvolio. And then to have the humour of state; and after a demure travel of regard, telling them I

know my place as I would they should do theirs,
to ask for my kinsman Toby,—

Sir Toby. Bolts and shackles!

Fabian. O, peace, peace, peace! now, now.

Malvolio. Seven of my people, with an obedient
start, make out for him: I frown the while, and
perchance wind up my watch, or play with my—
some rich jewel. Toby approaches; courtesies
there to me,—

Sir Toby. Shall this fellow live?

Fabian. Though our silence be drawn from us with
cars, yet peace.

Malvolio. I extend my hand to him thus, quenching
my familiar smile with an austere regard of con-
trol,—

Sir Toby. And does not Toby take you a blow o' the
lips then.

Malvolio. Saying, 'Cousin Toby, my fortunes having
cast me on your niece give me this prerogative
of speech,'—

Sir Toby. What, what?

Malvolio. 'You must amend your drunkenness.'

Sir Toby. Out, scab!

Fabian. Nay, patience, or we break the sinews of our
plot.

Malvolio. 'Besides, you waste the treasure of your
time, with a foolish knight,'—

Sir Andrew. That's me, I warrant you.

Malvolio. 'One Sir Andrew,'—

Sir Andrew. I knew 'twas I, for many do call me fool.

Malvolio. What employment have we here?

Taking up the letter

Sir Toby. Now is the woodcock near the gin.

Fabian. O, peace! and the spirit of humours intimate
reading aloud to him.

Malvolio. By my life, this is my lady's hand: these be her very c's, her u's, and her t's; and thus makes she her great P's. It is, in contempt of question, her hand.

Sir Andrew. Her c's, her u's and her t's: why that?

Malvolio. (*reads*) 'To the unknown belov'd, this, and my good wishes':—her very phrases! By your leave, wax. Soft! and the impressure her Lucrece, with which she uses to seal: 'tis my lady. To whom should this be?

Fabian. This wins, him, liver and all.

Malvolio. (*reads*) Jove knows I love:
But who?
Lips, do not move;
No man must know.

'No man must know.' What follows? the numbers altered! 'No man must know:' if this should be thee, Malvolio?

Sir Toby. Marry, hang thee, brock!

Malvolio. (*reads*)
I may command where I adore;
But silence, like a Lucrece knife,
With bloodless stroke my heart doth gore:
M, O, A, I, doth sway my life.

Fabian. A fustian riddle!

Sir Toby. Excellent wench, say I.

Malvolio. 'M, O, A, I, doth sway my life.' Nay, but first, let me see, let me see, let me see.

Fabian. What dish o' poison has she dressed him!

Sir Toby. And with what wing the staniel checks at it!

Malvolio. 'I may command where I adore.' Why, she may command me: I serve her, she is my lady. Why, this is evident to any formal capacity; there is no obstruction in this: and the end,—what

should that alphabetical position portend? If I
could make that resemble something in me,—
Softly! M, O, A, I,—

Sir Toby. O, ay, make up that: he is now at a cold
scent.

Fabian. Sowter will cry upon 't for all this, though it
be as rank as a fox.

Malvolio. M,—Malvolio; M,—why, that begins my
name.

Fabian. Did not I say he would work it out? the cur
is excellent at faults.

Malvolio. M,—but then there is no consonancy in the
sequel that suffers under probation: A should follow, but O does.

Fabian. And O shall end, I hope.

Sir Toby. Ay, or I'll cudgel him, and make him cry O!

Malvolio. And then I comes behind.

Fabian. Ay, an you had any eye behind you, you
might see more detraction at your heels than fortunes before you.

Malvolio. M, O, A, I; this simulation is not as the
former: and yet, to crush this a little, it would bow
to me, for every one of these letters are in my
name. Soft! here follows prose.
    (*reads*) If this fall into thy hand, revolve. In my
stars I am above thee, but be not afraid of greatness: some are born great, some achieve greatness, and some have greatness thrust upon 'em.
Thy Fates open their hands; let thy blood and
spirit embrace them; and, to inure thyself to what
thou art like to be, cast thy humble slough and
appear fresh. Be opposite with a kinsman, surly
with servants; let thy tongue tang arguments of
state; put thyself into the trick of singularity: she
thus advises thee that sighs for thee. Remember

who commended thy yellow stockings, and wish'd to see thee ever cross-garter'd: I say, remember. Go to, thou art made, if thou desirest to be so; if not, let me see thee a steward still, the fellow of servants, and not worthy to touch Fortune's fingers. Farewell. She that would alter services with thee,

THE FORTUNATE-UNHAPPY.

Daylight and champain discovers not more: this is open. I will be proud, I will read politic authors, I will baffle Sir Toby, I will wash off gross acquaintance, I will be point-devise the very man. I do not now fool myself, to let imagination jade me; for every reason excites to this, that my lady loves me. She did commend my yellow stockings of late, she did praise my leg being cross-garter'd, and in this she manifests herself to my love, and with a kind of injunction drives me to these habits of her liking. I thank my stars, I am happy. I will be strange, stout, in yellow stockings, and cross-garter'd, even with the swiftness of putting on. Jove and my stars be praised! Here is yet a postscript. (*reads*) Thou canst not choose but know who I am. If thou entertainest my love, let it appear in thy smiling; thy smiles become thee well; therefore in my presence still smile, dear my sweet, I prithee. Jove, I thank thee, I will smile, I will do everything that thou wilt have me. *Exit Fabian.* I will not give my part of this sport for a pension of thousands to be paid from the Sophy.

Sir Toby. I could marry this wench for this device,—

Sir Andrew. So could I too.

Sir Toby. And ask no other dowry with her but such another jest.

Sir Andrew. Nor I neither.

Fabian. Here comes my noble gull-catcher.

Re-enter Maria

Sir Toby. Wilt thou set thy foot o' my neck?

Sir Andrew. Or o' mine either?

Sir Toby. Shall I play my freedom at tray-trip, and become thy bond-slave?

Sir Andrew. I' faith, or I either?

Sir Toby. Why, thou hast put him in such a dream, that when the image of it leaves him he must run mad.

Maria. Nay, but say true, does it work upon him?

Sir Toby. Like aqua-vitæ with a midwife.

Maria. If you will then see the fruits of the sport, mark his first approach before my lady: he will come to her in yellow stockings, and 'tis a colour she abhors, and cross-garter'd, a fashion she detests; and he will smile upon her, which will now be so unsuitable to her disposition, being addicted to a melancholy as she is, that it cannot but turn him into a notable contempt. If you will see it, follow me.

Sir Toby. To the gates of Tartar, thou most excellent devil of wit!

Sir Andrew. I'll make one too.   *Exeunt*

ACT III

SCENE I

Olivia's garden

Enter Viola, and Clown with a tabor

Viola. Save thee, friend, and thy music: dost thou live by thy tabor?

Feste. No, sir, I live by the church.

Viola. Art thou a churchman?

Feste. No such matter, sir: I do live by the church, for I do live at my house, and my house doth stand by the church.

Viola. So thou mayst say, the king lies by a beggar, if a beggar dwell near him; or, the church stands by thy tabor, if thy tabor stand by the church.

Feste. You have said, sir. To see this age! A sentence is but a cheveril glove to a good wit: how quickly the wrong side may be turned outward!

Viola. Nay, that's certain; they that dally nicely with words may quickly make them wanton.

Feste. I would, therefore, my sister had had no name, sir.

Viola. Why, man?

Feste. Why, sir, her name's a word; and to dally with that word might make my sister wanton.

But indeed words are very rascals since bonds disgrac'd them.

Viola. Thy reason, man?

Feste. Troth, sir, I can yield you none without words; and words are grown so false, I am loath to prove reason with them.

Viola. I warrant thou art a merry fellow, and carest for nothing.

Feste. Not so, sir, I do care for something; but in my conscience, sir, I do not care for you: if that be to care for nothing, sir, I would it would make you invisible.

Viola. Art not thou the Lady Olivia's fool?

Feste. No, indeed, sir; the Lady Olivia has no folly: she will keep no fool, sir, till she be married, and fools are as like husbands as pilchards are to herrings; the husband's the bigger: I am indeed not her fool, but her corrupter of words.

Viola. I saw thee late at the Count Orsino's.

Feste. Foolery, sir, does walk about the orb like the sun, it shines every where. I would be sorry, sir, but the fool should be as oft with your master as with my mistress: I think I saw your wisdom there.

Viola. Nay, an thou pass upon me, I'll no more with thee. Hold, there's expenses for thee.

Feste. Now Jove, in his next commodity of hair, send thee a beard!

Viola. By my troth, I'll tell thee, I am almost sick for one; (*aside*) though I would not have it grow on my chin. Is thy lady within?

Feste. Would not a pair of these have bred, sir?

Viola. Yes, being kept together and put to use.

Feste. I would play Lord Pandarus of Phrygia, sir, to bring a Cressida to this Troilus.

Viola. I understand you, sir; 'tis well begg'd.

Feste. The matter, I hope, is not great, sir, begging
but a beggar: Cressida was a beggar. My lady is
within, sir. I will conster to them whence you
come; who you are, and what you would, are out
of my welkin, I might say 'element,' but the word
is over-worn. *Exit*

Viola. This fellow is wise enough to play the fool;
And to do that well craves a kind of wit:
He must observe their mood on whom he jests,
The quality of persons, and the time,
And, like the haggard, check at every feather
That comes before his eye. This is a practice
As full of labour as a wise man's art:
For folly that he wisely shows is fit;
But wise men, folly-fall'n, quite taint their wit.

Enter Sir Toby, and Sir Andrew

Sir Toby. Save you, gentleman.

Viola. And you, sir.

Sir Andrew. Dieu vous garde, monsieur.

Viola. Et vous aussi; votre serviteur.

Sir Andrew. I hope, sir, you are; and I am yours.

Sir Toby. Will you encounter the house? my niece
is desirous you should enter, if your trade be to
her.

Viola. I am bound to your niece, sir; I mean, she is
the list of my voyage.

Sir Toby. Taste your legs, sir, put them to motion.

Viola. My legs do better understand me, sir, than I
understand what you mean by bidding me taste
my legs.

Sir Toby. I mean, to go, sir, to enter.

Viola. I will answer you with gait and entrance. But
we are prevented.

Enter Olivia and Maria

Most excellent accomplish'd lady, the heavens
rain odours on you!

Sir Andrew. That youth 's a rare courtier: 'Rain
odours;' well.

Viola. My matter hath no voice, lady, but to your
own most pregnant and vouchsafed ear.

Sir Andrew. 'Odours,' 'pregnant,' and 'vouchsafed:'
I'll get 'em all three all ready.

Olivia. Let the garden door be shut, and leave me
to my hearing. (*exeunt Sir Toby, Sir Andrew, and
Maria.*) Give me your hand, sir.

Viola. My duty, madam, and most humble service.

Olivia. What is your name?

Viola. Cesario is your servant's name, fair princess.

Olivia. My servant, sir? 'Twas never merry world
Since lowly feigning was call'd compliment:
You're servant to the Count Orsino, youth.

Viola. And he is yours, and his must needs be yours:
Your servant's servant is your servant, madam.

Olivia. For him, I think not on him: for his thoughts,
Would they were blanks, rather than fill'd with
me!

Viola. Madam, I come to whet your gentle thoughts
On his behalf.

Olivia.   O, by your leave, I pray you;
I bade you never speak again of him:
But, would you undertake another suit,
I had rather hear you to solicit that
Than music from the spheres.

Viola.   Dear lady,—

Olivia. Give me leave, beseech you. I did send,
After the last enchantment you did here,
A ring in chase of you: so did I abuse

Myself, my servant and, I fear me, you:
Under your hard construction must I sit,
To force that on you, in a shameful cunning,
Which you knew none of yours: what might
you think?
Have you not set mine honour at the stake
And baited it with all the unmuzzled thoughts
That tyrannous heart can think? To one of your
receiving
Enough is shown; a cypress, not a bosom,
Hides my heart. So, let me hear you speak.
Viola. I pity you.
Olivia.   That's a degree to love.
Viola. No, not a grize; for 'tis a vulgar proof,
That very oft we pity enemies.
Olivia. Why, then, methinks 'tis time to smile again.
O world, how apt the poor are to be proud!
If one should be a prey, how much the better
To fall before the lion than the wolf!
                    Clock strikes
The clock upbraids me with the waste of time.
Be not afraid, good youth, I will not have you:
And yet, when wit and youth is come to harvest,
Your wife is like to reap a proper man;
There lies your way, due west.
Viola.   Then westward-ho!
Grace and good disposition attend your ladyship!
You'll nothing, madam, to my lord by me?
Olivia. Stay:
I prithee, tell me what thou think'st of me.
Viola. That you do think you are not what you are.
Olivia. If I think so, I think the same of you.
Viola. Then think you right: I am not what I am.
Olivia. I would you were as I would have you be!
Viola. Would it be better, madam, than I am?

I wish it might, for now I am your fool.
Olivia. O, what a deal of scorn looks beautiful
   In the contempt and anger of his lip!
   A murderous guilt shows not itself more soon
   Than love that would seem hid: love's night is
      noon.
   Cesario, by the roses of the spring,
   By maidhood, honour, truth and every thing,
   I love thee so, that, maugre all thy pride,
   Nor wit nor reason can my passion hide.
   Do not extort thy reasons from this clause,
   For that I woo, thou therefore hast no cause;
   But rather reason thus with reason fetter,
   Love sought is good, but given unsought is better.
Viola. By innocence I swear, and by my youth,
   I have one heart, one bosom, and one truth,
   And that no woman has, nor never none
   Shall mistress be of it, save I alone.
   And so adieu, good madam: never more
   Will I my master's tears to you deplore.
Olivia. Yet come again; for thou perhaps mayst
      move.
   That heart, which now abhors, to like his love.
                                            Exeunt

SCENE II

Olivia's house

Enter Sir Toby, Sir Andrew, and Fabian

Sir Andrew. No, faith, I'll not stay a jot longer.

Sir Toby. Thy reason, dear venom, give thy reason.

Fabian. You must needs yield your reason, Sir Andrew.

Sir Andrew. Marry, I saw your niece do more favours to the count's serving-man than ever she bestow'd upon me; I saw 't i' the orchard.

Sir Toby. Did she see thee the while, old boy? tell me that.

Sir Andrew. As plain as I see you now.

Fabian. This was a great argument of love in her toward you.

Sir Andrew. 'Slight, will you make an ass o' me?

Fabian. I will prove it legitimate, sir, upon the oaths of judgement and reason.

Sir Toby. And they have been grand-jurymen since before Noah was a sailor.

Fabian. She did show favour to the youth in your sight only to exasperate you, to awake your dormouse valour, to put fire in your heart, and brimstone in your liver. You should then have accosted her, and with some excellent jests, fire-new from the mint, you should have bang'd the youth into dumbness. This was look'd for at your hand, and this was balk'd: the double gilt of this opportunity you let time wash off, and you are now sail'd into the north of my lady's opinion, where you will hang like an icicle on a Dutch-man's beard, unless you do redeem it by some laudable attempt, either of valour or policy.

Sir Andrew. An 't be any way, it must be with valour, for policy I hate: I had as lief be a Brownist as a politician.

Sir Toby. Why, then, build me thy fortunes upon the basis of valour. Challenge me the count's youth to fight with him; hurt him in eleven places, my niece shall take note of it, and assure thyself, there is no love-broker in the world can more prevail in man's commendation with woman than report of valour.

Fabian. There is no way but this, Sir Andrew.

Sir Andrew. Will either of you bear me a challenge to him?

Sir Toby. Go, write it in a martial hand, be curst and brief; it is no matter how witty, so it be eloquent, and full of invention: taunt him with the license of ink: if thou thou 'st him some thrice, it shall not be amiss, and as many lies as will lie in thy sheet of paper, although the sheet were big enough for the bed of Ware in England, set 'em down, go about it. Let there be gall enough in thy ink, though thou write with a goose-pen, no matter: about it.

Sir Andrew. Where shall I find you?

Sir Toby. We'll call thee at the cubicle: go.

Exit Sir Andrew

Fabian. This is a dear manakin to you, Sir Toby.

Sir Toby. I have been dear to him, lad, some two thousand strong, or so.

Fabian. We shall have a rare letter from him: but you'll not deliver 't?

Sir Toby. Never trust me, then; and by all means stir on the youth to an answer. I think oxen and wainropes cannot hale them together. For Andrew, if he were open'd, and you find so much blood in his liver as will clog the foot of a flea, I'll eat the rest of the anatomy.

Fabian. And his opposite, the youth, bears in his visage no great presage of cruelty.

Enter Maria

Sir Toby. Look, where the youngest wren of nine comes.

Maria. If you desire the spleen, and will laugh yourselves into stitches, follow me. Yond gull Malvolio is turned heathen, a very renegado; for there is no Christian, that means to be saved by believing rightly, can ever believe such impossible passages of grossness. He's in yellow stockings.

Sir Toby. And cross-gartered?

Maria. Most villanously; like a pedant that keeps a school i' the church. I have dogg'd him like his murderer. He does obey every point of the letter that I dropp'd to betray him: he does smile his face into more lines than is in the new map with the augmentation of the Indies: you have not seen such a thing as 'tis. I can hardly forbear hurling things at him. I know my lady will strike him: if she do, he'll smile and take 't for a great favour.

Sir Toby. Come, bring us, bring us where he is.

Exeunt

SCENE III

A street

Enter Sebastian and Antonio

Sebastian. I would not by my will have troubled
    you,
  But, since you make your pleasure of your pains,
  I will no further chide you.
Antonio. I could not stay behind you: my desire,
  More sharp than filed steel, did spur me forth,
  And not all love to see you, though so much
  As might have drawn one to a longer voyage,
  But jealousy what might befall your travel,
  Being skilless in these parts; which to a stranger,
  Unguided, and unfriended, often prove
  Rough, and unhospitable: my willing love,
  The rather by these arguments of fear,
  Set forth in your pursuit.
Sebastian.   My kind Antonio,
  I can no other answer make but thanks,
  And thanks, and ever thanks; how oft good turns
  Are shuffled off with such uncurrent pay:
  But, were my worth as is my conscience firm,
  You should find better dealing. What's to do?
  Shall we go see the reliques of this town?
Antonio. To-morrow, sir: best first go see your lodg-
    ing.
Sebastian. I am not weary, and 'tis long to night:
  I pray you, let us satisfy our eyes
  With the memorials and the things of fame
  That do renown this city.
Antonio.   Would you 'ld pardon me;
  I do not without danger walk these streets:
  Once in a sea-fight 'gainst the count his galleys

I did some service, of such note indeed,
That were I ta'en here it would scarce be answer'd.

Sebastian. Belike you slew great number of his people.

Antonio. The offence is not of such a bloody nature,
Albeit the quality of the time and quarrel
Might well have given us bloody argument.
It might have since been answer'd in repaying
What we took from them; which, for traffic's sake,
Most of our city did: only myself stood out,
For which, if I be lapsed in this place,
I shall pay dear.

Sebastian.   Do not then walk too open.

Antonio. It doth not fit me. Hold, sir, here's my purse.
In the south suburbs, at the Elephant,
Is best to lodge: I will bespeak our diet,
Whiles you beguile the time and feed your knowledge
With viewing of the town: there shall you have me.

Sebastian. Why I your purse?

Antonio. Haply your eye shall light upon some toy
You have some desire to purchase; and your store,
I think, is not for idle markets, sir.

Sebastian. I'll be your purse-bearer and leave you
For an hour.

Antonio.   To the Elephant.

Sebastian.   I do remember. *Exeunt*

SCENE IV

Olivia's garden

Enter Olivia and Maria

Olivia. I have sent after him, he says he'll come;
How shall I feast him? what bestow of him?
For youth is bought more oft than begg'd or
borrow'd.
I speak too loud.
Where is Malvolio? he is sad and civil,
And suits well for a servant with my fortunes:
Where is Malvolio?

Maria. He's coming, madam; but in very strange
manner.
He is sure possess'd, madam.

Olivia. Why, what's the matter? does he rave?

Maria. No, madam, he does nothing but smile: your
ladyship were best to have some guard about
you, if he come, for sure the man is tainted in 's
wits.

Olivia. Go call him hither. (*exit Maria.*) I am as
mad as he,
If sad and merry madness equal be.

Re-enter Maria, with Malvolio

How now, Malvolio?

Malvolio. Sweet lady, ho, ho.

Olivia. Smilest thou?
I sent for thee upon a sad occasion.

Malvolio. Sad, lady? I could be sad: this does make
some obstruction in the blood, this cross-
gartering; but what of that? if it please the eye of
one, it is with me as the very true sonnet is,
'Please one, and please all.'

Olivia. Why, how dost thou, man? what is the matter with thee?

Malvolio. Not black in my mind, though yellow in my legs. It did come to his hands, and commands shall be executed: I think we do know the sweet Roman hand.

Olivia. Wilt thou go to bed, Malvolio?

Malvolio. To bed! ay, sweet-heart, and I'll come to thee.

Olivia. God comfort thee! Why dost thou smile so and kiss thy hand so oft?

Maria. How do you, Malvolio?

Malvolio. At your request! yes; nightingales answer daws.

Maria. Why appear you with this ridiculous boldness before my lady?

Malvolio. 'Be not afraid of greatness:' 'twas well writ.

Olivia. What mean'st thou by that, Malvolio?

Malvolio. 'Some are born great,'—

Olivia. Ha?

Malvolio. 'Some achieve greatness,'—

Olivia. What say'st thou?

Malvolio. 'And some have greatness thrust upon them.'

Olivia. Heaven restore thee!

Malvolio. 'Remember who commended thy yellow stockings,'—

Olivia. My yellow stockings?

Malvolio. 'And wish'd to see thee cross-gartered.'

Olivia. Cross-gartered?

Malvolio. 'Go to, thou art made, if thou desir'st to be so;'—

Olivia. Am I made?

Malvolio. 'If not, let me see thee a servant still.'

Olivia. Why, this is very midsummer madness.

Enter Servant

Servant. Madam, the young gentleman of the
Count Orsino's is return'd: I could hardly entreat
him back: he attends your ladyship's pleasure.

Olivia. I'll come to him. (*exit Servant.*) Good
Maria, let this fellow be look'd to. Where's my
cousin Toby? Let some of my people have a
special care of him: I would not have him mis-
carry for the half of my dowry.

Exeunt Olivia and Maria

Malvolio. O, ho! do you come near me now? no
worse man than Sir Toby to look to me! This con-
curs directly with the letter: she sends him on
purpose, that I may appear stubborn to him; for
she incites me to that in the letter. 'Cast thy
humble slough,' says she; 'be opposite with a kinsman, surly with servants, let thy tongue tang
with arguments of state, put thyself into the trick
of singularity;' and consequently sets down the
manner how; as, a sad face, a reverend carriage,
a slow tongue, in the habit of some sir of note, and
so forth. I have lim'd her, but it is Jove's doing,
and Jove make me thankful! And when she went
away now, 'Let this fellow be look'd to:' fellow?
not Malvolio, nor after my degree, but fellow.
Why, every thing adheres together, that no dram
of a scruple, no scruple of a scruple, no obstacle,
no incredulous or unsafe circumstance—What can
be said? Nothing that can be can come between
me and the full prospect of my hopes. Well, Jove,
not I, is the doer of this, and he is to be thanked.

Re-enter Maria, with Sir Toby and Fabian

Sir Toby. Which way is he, in the name of sanctity?
If all the devils of hell be drawn in little, and
Legion himself possess'd him, yet I'll speak to him.

Fabian. Here he is, here he is. How is 't with you, sir? how is 't with you, man?

Malvolio. Go off, I discard you: let me enjoy my private: go off.

Maria. Lo, how hollow the fiend speaks within him! did not I tell you? Sir Toby, my lady prays you to have a care of him.

Malvolio. Ah, ha! does she so?

Sir Toby. Go to, go to; peace, peace, we must deal gently with him; let me alone. How do you, Malvolio? how is 't with you? What, man! defy the devil: consider, he's an enemy to mankind.

Malvolio. Do you know what you say?

Maria. La you, an you speak ill of the devil, how he takes it at heart! Pray God, he be not bewitch'd!

Fabian. Carry his water to the wise woman.

Maria. Marry, and it shall be done to-morrow morning, if I live. My lady would not lose him for more than I'll say.

Malvolio. How now, mistress?

Maria. O Lord!

Sir Toby. Prithee, hold thy peace, this is not the way: do you not see you move him? let me alone with him.

Fabian. No way but gentleness, gently, gently: the fiend is rough, and will not be roughly us'd.

Sir Toby. Why, how now, my bawcock! how dost thou, chuck?

Malvolio. Sir!

Sir Toby. Ay, Biddy, come with me. What, man, 'tis not for gravity to play at cherry-pit with Satan: hang him, foul collier!

Maria. Get him to say his prayers, good Sir Toby, get him to pray.

Malvolio. My prayers, minx?

Maria. No, I warrant you, he will not hear of godliness.

Malvolio. Go, hang yourselves all! you are idle shallow things: I am not of your element: you shall know more hereafter.   *Exit*

Sir Toby. Is 't possible?

Fabian. If this were played upon a stage now, I could condemn it as an improbable fiction.

Sir Toby. His very genius hath taken the infection of the device, man.

Maria. Nay, pursue him now, lest the device take air and taint.

Fabian. Why, we shall make him mad indeed.

Maria. The house will be the quieter.

Sir Toby. Come, we'll have him in a dark room and bound. My niece is already in the belief that he's mad: we may carry it thus, for our pleasure and his penance, till our very pastime, tired out of breath, prompt us to have mercy on him: at which time we will bring the device to the bar and crown thee for a finder of madmen. But see, but see.

Enter Sir Andrew

Fabian. More matter for a May morning.

Sir Andrew. Here's the challenge, read it: I warrant there's vinegar and pepper in 't.

Fabian. Is 't so saucy?

Sir Andrew. Ay, is 't, I warrant him: do but read.

Sir Toby. Give me. (*reads*) Youth, whatsoever thou art, thou art but a scurvy fellow.

Fabian. Good, and valiant.

Sir Toby. (*reads*) Wonder not, nor admire not in thy mind, why I do call thee so, for I will show thee no reason for 't.

Fabian. A good note, that keeps you from the blow of the law.

Sir Toby. (*reads*) Thou comest to the lady Olivia, and in my sight she uses thee kindly: but thou liest in thy throat; that is not the matter I challenge thee for.

Fabian. Very brief, and to exceeding good senseless.

Sir Toby. (*reads*) I will waylay thee going home; where if it be thy chance to kill me,—

Fabian. Good.

Sir Toby. (*reads*) Thou kill'st me like a rogue and a villain.

Fabian. Still you keep o' the windy side of the law: good.

Sir Toby. (*reads*) Fare thee well, and God have mercy upon one of our souls! He may have mercy upon mine, but my hope is better, and so look to thyself. Thy friend, as thou usest him, and thy sworn enemy,

ANDREW AGUECHEEK.

If this letter move him not, his legs cannot: I'll give 't him.

Maria. You may have very fit occasion for 't: he is now in some commerce with my lady, and will by and by depart.

Sir Toby. Go, Sir Andrew; scout me for him at the corner of the orchard like a bum-baily: so soon as ever thou seest him, draw, and, as thou draw'st, swear horrible; for it comes to pass oft that a terrible oath, with a swaggering accent sharply twang'd off, gives manhood more approbation than ever proof itself would have earn'd him. Away!

Sir Andrew. Nay, let me alone for swearing. *Exit*

Sir Toby. Now will not I deliver his letter: for the

behaviour of the young gentleman gives him out
to be of good capacity and breeding; his employment between his lord and my niece confirms
no less: therefore this letter, being so excellently
ignorant, will breed no terror in the youth: he
will find it comes from a clodpole. But, sir, I will
deliver his challenge by word of mouth; set upon
Aguecheek a notable report of valour, and drive
the gentleman (as I know his youth will aptly
receive it) into a most hideous opinion of his
rage, skill, fury, and impetuosity. This will so
fright them both, that they will kill one another
by the look, like cockatrices.

Re-enter Olivia, with Viola

Fabian. Here he comes with your niece, give them
way till he take leave, and presently after him.

Sir Toby. I will meditate the while upon some hor-
rid message for a challenge.

Exeunt Sir Toby, Fabian, and Maria

Olivia. I have said too much unto a heart of stone,
And laid mine honour too unchary out:
There's something in me that reproves my fault;
But such a headstrong potent fault it is,
That it but mocks reproof.

Viola. With the same 'haviour that your passion
bears
Goes on my master's grief.

Olivia. Here, wear this jewel for me, 'tis my picture;
Refuse it not, it hath no tongue to vex you;
And I beseech you come again to-morrow.
What shall you ask of me that I'll deny,
That honour sav'd may upon asking give?

Viola. Nothing but this;—your true love for my
master.

Olivia. How with mine honour may I give him that

Which I have given to you?

Viola. I will acquit you.

Olivia. Well, come again to-morrow: fare thee well:
A fiend like thee might bear my soul to hell. *Exit*

Re-enter Sir Toby and Fabian

Sir Toby. Gentleman, God save thee.

Viola. And you, sir.

Sir Toby. That defence thou hast, betake thee to 't:
of what nature the wrongs are thou hast done
him, I know not; but thy intercepter, full of
despite, bloody as the hunter, attends thee at the
orchard-end: dismount thy tuck, be yare in thy
preparation, for thy assailant is quick, skilful, and
deadly.

Viola. You mistake, sir; I am sure no man hath any
quarrel to me: my remembrance is very free and
clear from any image of offence done to any man.

Sir Toby. You'll find it otherwise, I assure you:
therefore, if you hold your life at any price, betake you to your guard; for your opposite hath in
him what youth, strength, skill and wrath can
furnish man withal.

Viola. I pray you, sir, what is he?

Sir Toby. He is knight, dubb'd with unhatched
rapier and on carpet consideration; but he is a
devil in private brawl: souls and bodies hath he
divorc'd three; and his incensement at this mo-
ment is so implacable, that satisfaction can be
none but by pangs of deaths and sepulchre. Hob,
nob, is his word; give 't or take 't.

Viola. I will return again into the house, and desire
some conduct of the lady. I am no fighter. I have
heard of some kind of men that put quarrels pur-
posely on others, to taste their valour: belike this
is a man of that quirk.

Sir Toby. Sir, no; his indignation derives itself out of a very competent injury, therefore, get you on, and give him his desire. Back you shall not to the house, unless you undertake that with me which with as much safety you might answer him: therefore, on, or strip your sword stark naked; for meddle you must, that's certain, or forswear to wear iron about you.

Viola. This is as uncivil as strange. I beseech you, do me this courteous office, as to know of the knight what my offence to him is: it is something of my negligence, nothing of my purpose.

Sir Toby. I will do so. Signior Fabian, stay you by this gentleman till my return.   *Exit*

Viola. Pray you, sir, do you know of this matter?

Fabian. I know the knight is incens'd against you, even to a mortal arbitrement, but nothing of the circumstance more.

Viola. I beseech you, what manner of man is he?

Fabian. Nothing of that wonderful promise, to read him by his form, as you are like to find him in the proof of his valour. He is, indeed, sir, the most skilful, bloody, and fatal opposite that you could possibly have found in any part of Illyria. Will you walk towards him? I will make your peace with him if I can.

Viola. I shall be much bound to you for 't: I am one that had rather go with sir priest than sir knight: I care not who knows so much of my mettle.

                                        Exeunt

Re-enter Sir Toby, with Sir Andrew

Sir Toby. Why, man, he's a very devil; I have not seen such a firago. I had a pass with him, rapier, scabbard and all, and he gives me the stuck in

with such a mortal motion, that it is inevitable;
and on the answer, he pays you as surely as your
feet hit the ground they step on. They say he has
been fencer to the Sophy.

Sir Andrew. Pox on 't, I'll not meddle with him.

Sir Toby. Ay, but he will not now be pacified:
Fabian can scarce hold him yonder.

Sir Andrew. Plague on 't, an I thought he had been
valiant, and so cunning in fence, I 'ld have seen
him damn'd ere I 'ld have challeng'd him. Let
him let the matter slip, and I'll give him my horse,
grey Capilet.

Sir Toby. I'll make the motion: stand here, make a
good show on 't, this shall end without the perdi-
tion of souls. (*aside*) Marry, I'll ride your horse
as well as I ride you.

Re-enter Fabian and Viola

(*to Fabian*) I have his horse to take up the quarrel: I have persuaded him the youth's a devil.

Fabian. He is as horribly conceited of him; and
pants and looks pale, as if a bear were at his heels.

Sir Toby. (*to Viola*) There's no remedy, sir; he will
fight with you for 's oath sake: marry, he hath
better bethought him of his quarrel, and he finds
that now scarce to be worth talking of: therefore
draw, for the supportance of his vow; he protests
he will not hurt you.

Viola. (*aside*) Pray God defend me! A little thing
would make me tell them how much I lack of a
man.

Fabian. Give ground, if you see him furious.

Sir Toby. Come, Sir Andrew, there's no remedy;
the gentleman will, for his honour's sake, have
one bout with you; he cannot by the duello avoid
it: but he has promis'd me, as he is a gentleman

and a soldier, he will not hurt you. Come on;
to 't.

Sir Andrew. Pray God, he keep his oath!

Viola. I do assure you, 'tis against my will.

They draw

Enter Antonio

Antonio. Put up your sword. If this young gentle-
man
Have done offence, I take the fault on me:
If you offend him, I for him defy you.

Sir Toby. You, sir? why, what are you?

Antonio. One, sir, that for his love dares yet do
more
Than you have heard him brag to you he will.

Sir Toby. Nay, if you be an undertaker, I am for
you.   *They draw*

Enter Officers

Fabian. O good Sir Toby, hold! here comes the
officers.

Sir Toby. I'll be with you anon.

Viola. Pray, sir, put your sword up, if you please.

Sir Andrew. Marry, will I, sir; and, for that I prom-
ised you, I'll be as good as my word: he will bear
you easily, and reins well.

First Off. This is the man, do thy office.

Sec. Off. Antonio, I arrest thee at the suit of Count
Orsino.

Antonio. You do mistake me, sir.

First Off. No, sir, no jot; I know your favour well,
Though now you have no sea-cap on your head.
Take him away, he knows I know him well.

Antonio. I must obey. (*to Viola*) This comes with
seeking you:
But there's no remedy, I shall answer it.
What will you do, now my necessity

Makes me to ask you for my purse? It grieves me
Much more for what I cannot do for you
Than what befalls myself. You stand amaz'd,
But be of comfort.
Sec. Off. Come, sir, away.
Antonio. I must entreat of you some of that money.
Viola. What money, sir?
For the fair kindness you have show'd me here,
And part being prompted by your present trou-
ble,
Out of my lean and low ability
I'll lend you something: my having is not much;
I'll make division of my present with you:
Hold, there's half my coffer.
Antonio.   Will you deny me now?
Is 't possible that my deserts to you
Can lack persuasion? Do not tempt my misery,
Lest that it make me so unsound a man
As to upbraid you with those kindnesses
That I have done for you.
Viola.   I know of none;
Nor know I you by voice or any feature:
I hate ingratitude more in a man
Than lying vainness, babbling drunkenness,
Or any taint of vice whose strong corruption
Inhabits our frail blood.
Antonio.   O heavens themselves!
Sec. Off. Come, sir, I pray you, go.
Antonio. Let me speak a little. This youth that you
see here
I snatch'd one half out of the jaws of death:
Reliev'd him with such sanctity of love;
And to his image, which methought did promise
Most venerable worth, did I devotion.
First Off. What's that to us? The time goes by:
away!

Antonio. But how vile an idol proves this god!
Thou hast, Sebastian, done good feature shame,
In nature there's no blemish but the mind;
None can be call'd deform'd but the unkind:
Virtue is beauty; but the beauteous evil
Are empty trunks, o'erflourish'd by the devil.
First Off. The man grows mad: away with him!
Come, come, sir.
Antonio. Lead me on.   *Exit with Officers*
Viola. Methinks his words do from such passion fly,
That he believes himself: so do not I.
Prove true, imagination, O prove true,
That I, dear brother, be now ta'en for you!
Sir Toby. Come hither, knight; come hither, Fabian:
we'll whisper o'er a couplet or two of most sage
saws.
Viola. He nam'd Sebastian: I my brother know
Yet living in my glass; even such, and so
In favour was my brother, and he went
Still in this fashion, colour, ornament,
For him I imitate: O, if it prove,
Tempests are kind, and salt waves fresh in love!
                                                Exit
Sir Toby. A very dishonest paltry boy, and more a
coward than a hare: his dishonesty appears in
leaving his friend here in necessity, and denying
him; and for his cowardship, ask Fabian.
Fabian. A coward, a most devout coward, religious
in it.
Sir Andrew. 'Slid, I'll after him again and beat him.
Sir Toby. Do; cuff him soundly, but never draw thy
sword.
Sir Andrew. An I do not,—   *Exit*
Fabian. Come, let's see the event.
Sir Toby. I dare lay any money 'twill be nothing yet.
                                                Exeunt

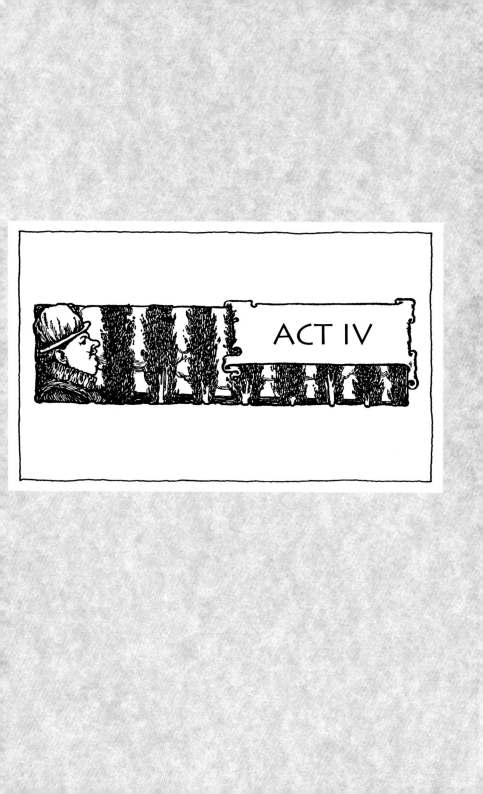

SCENE I

Before Olivia's house

Enter Sebastian and Clown

Feste. Will you make me believe that I am not sent
for you?

Sebastian. Go to, go to, thou art a foolish fellow:
Let me be clear of thee.

Feste. Well held out, i' faith! No, I do not know you,
nor I am not sent to you by my lady, to bid you
come speak with her; nor your name is not Master Cesario, nor this is not my nose neither. Nothing that is so is so.

Sebastian. I prithee, vent thy folly somewhere else:
Thou know'st not me.

Feste. Vent my folly! he has heard that word of
some great man, and now applies it to a fool.
Vent my folly! I am afraid this great lubber, the
world, will prove a cockney. I prithee now, un-
gird thy strangeness, and tell me what I shall vent
to my lady? shall I vent to her that thou art
coming?

Sebastian. I prithee, foolish Greek, depart from me:
There's money for thee: if you tarry longer,
I shall give worse payment.

Feste. By my troth, thou hast an open hand. These
wise men that give fools money get themselves a
good report—after fourteen years' purchase.

Enter Sir Andrew, Sir Toby, and Fabian

Sir Andrew. Now, sir, have I met you again? there's
for you.

Sebastian. Why, there's for thee, and there, and
there.

Are all the people mad?

Sir Toby. Hold, sir, or I'll throw your dagger o'er
the house.

Feste. This will I tell my lady straight: I would not
be in some of your coats for two pence.   *Exit*

Sir Toby. Come on, sir; hold.

Sir Andrew. Nay, let him alone: I'll go another way
to work with him; I'll have an action of battery
against him, if there be any law in Illyria: though
I struck him first, yet it's no matter for that.

Sebastian. Let go thy hand.

Sir Toby. Come, sir, I will not let you go. Come, my
young soldier, put up your iron: you are well
flesh'd; come on.

Sebastian. I will be free from thee. What wouldst
thou now?

If thou dar'st tempt me further, draw thy sword.

Sir Toby. What, what? Nay, then I must have an
ounce or two of this malapert blood from you.

Enter Olivia

Olivia. Hold, Toby; on thy life, I charge thee, hold!

Sir Toby. Madam!

Olivia. Will it be ever thus? Ungracious wretch,
Fit for the mountains and the barbarous caves,
Where manners ne'er were preach'd! out of my
sight!

Be not offended, dear Cesario.

Rudesby, be gone!
Exeunt Sir Toby, Sir Andrew, and Fabian
                   I prithee, gentle friend,
Let thy fair wisdom, not thy passion, sway
In this uncivil and unjust extent
Against thy peace. Go with me to my house,
And hear thou there how many fruitless pranks
This ruffian hath botch'd up, that thou thereby
Mayst smile at this: thou shalt not choose but go:
Do not deny. Beshrew his soul for me,
He started one poor heart of mine in thee.

Sebastian. What relish is in this? how runs the
    stream?
Or I am mad, or else this is a dream:
Let fancy still my sense in Lethe sleep;
If it be thus to dream, still let me sleep!

Olivia. Nay, come, I prithee: would thou 'ldst be
    rul'd by me!

Sebastian. Madam, I will.

Olivia.   O, say so, and so be!
                                 Exeunt

SCENE II

Olivia's house

Enter Maria and Clown

Maria. Nay, I prithee, put on this gown, and this beard, make him believe thou art Sir Topas the curate: do it quickly; I'll call Sir Toby the whilst.

Exit

Feste. Well, I'll put it on, and I will dissemble myself in 't, and I would I were the first that ever dissembled in such a gown. I am not tall enough to become the function well, nor lean enough to be thought a good student; but to be said an honest man and a good housekeeper goes as fairly as to say a careful man and a great scholar. The competitors enter.

Enter Sir Toby and Maria

Sir Toby. Jove bless thee, master Parson.

Feste. Bonos dies, Sir Toby: for, as the old hermit of Prague, that never saw pen and ink, very wittily said to a niece of King Gorboduc, 'That that is, is;' so I, being master Parson, am master Parson; for, what is 'that,' but 'that,' and 'is,' but 'is'?

Sir Toby. To him, Sir Topas.

Feste. What, ho, I say! peace in this prison!

Sir Toby. The knave counterfeits well; a good knave.

Malvolio. (*within*) Who calls there?

Feste. Sir Topas the curate, who comes to visit Malvolio the lunatic.

Malvolio. Sir Topas, Sir Topas, good Sir Topas go to my lady.

Feste. Out, hyperbolical fiend, how vexest thou this man! talkest thou nothing but of ladies?

Sir Toby. Well said, master Parson.

Malvolio. Sir Topas, never was man thus wronged: good Sir Topas, do not think I am mad: they have laid me here in hideous darkness.

Feste. Fie, thou dishonest Satan! I call thee by the most modest terms, for I am one of those gentle ones that will use the devil himself with courtesy: say'st thou that house is dark?

Malvolio. As hell, Sir Topas.

Feste. Why, it hath bay windows transparent as barricadoes, and the clearstories toward the south north are as lustrous as ebony; and yet complainest thou of obstruction?

Malvolio. I am not mad, Sir Topas, I say to you this house is dark.

Feste. Madman, thou errest: I say there is no darkness but ignorance, in which thou art more puzzled than the Egyptians in their fog.

Malvolio. I say this house is as dark as ignorance, though ignorance were as dark as hell; and I say there was never man thus abus'd. I am no more mad than you are: make the trial of it in any constant question.

Feste. What is the opinion of Pythagoras concerning wild fowl?

Malvolio. That the soul of our grandam might haply inhabit a bird.

Feste. What thinkst thou of his opinion?

Malvolio. I think nobly of the soul, and no way approve his opinion.

Feste. Fare thee well. Remain thou still in darkness: thou shalt hold the opinion of Pythagoras ere I will allow of thy wits, and fear to kill a woodcock, lest thou dispossess the soul of thy grandam. Fare thee well.

Malvolio. Sir Topas, Sir Topas!

Sir Toby. My most exquisite Sir Topas!

Feste. Nay, I am for all waters.

Maria. Thou mightst have done this without thy beard and gown, he sees thee not.

Sir Toby. To him in thine own voice, and bring me word how thou findest him: I would we were well rid of this knavery. If he may be conveniently deliver'd, I would he were, for I am now so far in offence with my niece, that I cannot pursue with any safety this sport to the upshot. Come by and by to my chamber.   *Exeunt Sir Toby and Maria*

Feste. (*singing*) Hey, Robin, jolly Robin,
　　　　　　　　Tell me how thy lady does.

Malvolio. Fool,—

Feste. My lady is unkind, perdy.

Malvolio. Fool,—

Feste. Alas, why is she so?

Malvolio. Fool, I say,—

Feste. She loves another—Who calls, ha?

Malvolio. Good fool, as ever thou wilt deserve well at my hand, help me to a candle, and pen, ink, and paper: as I am a gentleman, I will live to be thankful to thee for 't.

Feste. Master Malvolio,—

Malvolio. Ay, good fool.

Feste. Alas, sir, how fell you besides your five wits?

Malvolio. Fool, there was never man so notoriously abus'd: I am as well in my wits, fool, as thou art.

Feste. But as well? then you are mad indeed, if you be no better in your wits than a fool.

Malvolio. They have here propertied me; keep me in darkness, send ministers to me, asses, and do all they can to face me out of my wits.

Feste. Advise you what you say; the minister is

here. Malvolio, Malvolio, thy wits the heavens restore! endeavour thyself to sleep, and leave thy
vain bibble babble.

Malvolio. Sir Topas,—

Feste. Maintain no words with him, good fellow.
Who, I, sir? not I, sir. God be wi' you, good Sir
Topas. Marry, amen. I will, sir, I will.

Malvolio. Fool, fool, fool, I say,—

Feste. Alas, sir, be patient. What say you, sir? I am
shent for speaking to you.

Malvolio. Good fool, help me to some light and
some paper: I tell thee, I am as well in my wits as
any man in Illyria.

Feste. Well-a-day, that you were, sir!

Malvolio. By this hand, I am. Good fool, some ink,
paper, and light; and convey what I will set down
to my lady: it shall advantage thee more than
ever the bearing of letter did.

Feste. I will help you to 't. But tell me true, are you
not mad indeed, or do you but counterfeit?

Malvolio. Believe me, I am not; I tell thee true.

Feste. Nay, I'll ne'er believe a madman till I see his
brains. I will fetch you light, and paper, and ink.

Malvolio. Fool, I'll requite it in the highest degree: I
prithee, be gone.

Feste. (*singing*) I am gone, sir,
   And anon, sir,
  I'll be with you again;
   In a trice,
   Like to the old vice,
  Your need to sustain;
  Who, with dagger of lath,
  In his rage and his wrath,
   Cries, ah, ha! to the devil;
  Like a mad lad,
  Pare thy nails, dad;
  Adieu, goodman devil.   *Exit*

SCENE III

Olivia's garden

Enter Sebastian

Sebastian. This is the air, that is the glorious sun,
This pearl she gave me, I do feel 't and see 't,
And though 'tis wonder that enwraps me thus,
Yet 'tis not madness. Where's Antonio, then?
I could not find him at the Elephant,
Yet there he was, and there I found this credit,
That he did range the town to seek me out.
His counsel now might do me golden service,
For though my soul disputes well with my sense,
That this may be some error, but no madness,
Yet doth this accident and flood of fortune
So far exceed all instance, all discourse,
That I am ready to distrust mine eyes
And wrangle with my reason, that persuades me
To any other trust but that I am mad,
Or else the lady's mad; yet, if 'twere so,
She could not sway her house, command her fol-
      lowers,
Take, and give back affairs, and their dispatch,
With such a smooth, discreet, and stable bearing
As I perceive she does: there's something in 't
That is deceivable. But here the lady comes.

Enter Olivia and Priest

Olivia. Blame not this haste of mine. If you mean
    well,
  Now go with me, and with this holy man
  Into the chantry by: there, before him,
  And underneath that consecrated roof,
  Plight me the full assurance of your faith,
  That my most jealous and too doubtful soul
  May live at peace. He shall conceal it
  Whiles you are willing it shall come to note,
  What time we will our celebration keep
  According to my birth. What do you say?
Sebastian. I'll follow this good man, and go with
    you,
  And having sworn truth, ever will be true.
Olivia. Then lead the way, good father; and heavens
    so shine,
  That they may fairly note this act of mine!

                               Exeunt

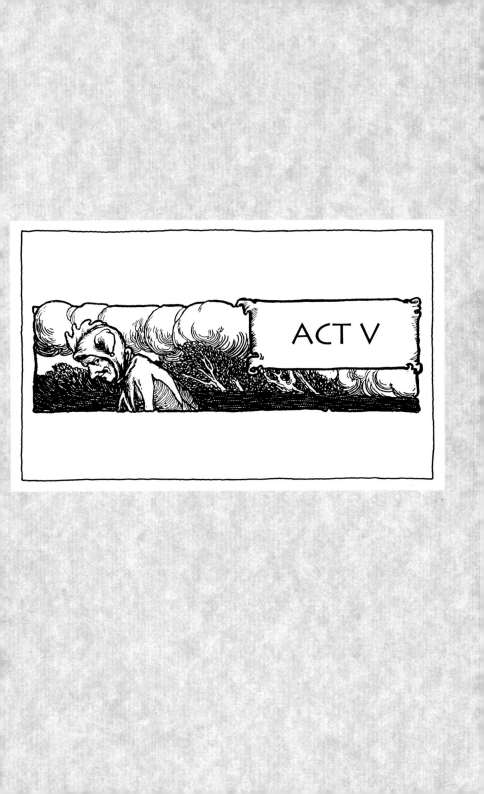

ACT V

SCENE I

Before Olivia's house

Enter Clown and Fabian

Fabian. Now, as thou lov'st me, let me see his letter.

Feste. Good Master Fabian, grant me another request.

Fabian. Any thing.

Feste. Do not desire to see this letter.

Fabian. This is, to give a dog, and in recompense desire my dog again.

Enter Duke, Viola, Curio, and Lords

Orsino. Belong you to the Lady Olivia, friends?

Feste. Ay, sir; we are some of her trappings.

Orsino. I know thee well: how dost thou, my good fellow?

Feste. Truly, sir, the better for my foes and the worse for my friends.

Orsino. Just the contrary; the better for thy friends.

Feste. No, sir, the worse.

Orsino. How can that be?

Feste. Marry, sir, they praise me and make an ass of me; now my foes tell me plainly, I am an ass: so that by my foes, sir, I profit in the knowledge of myself, and by my friends I am abused: so that, conclusions to be as kisses, if your four negatives make your two affirmatives, why then, the worse for my friends, and the better for my foes.

Orsino. Why, this is excellent.

Feste. By my troth, sir, no; though it please you to be one of my friends.

Orsino. Thou shalt not be the worse for me, there's gold.

Feste. But that it would be double-dealing, sir, I would you could make it another.

Orsino. O, you give me ill counsel.

Feste. Put your grace in your pocket, sir, for this once, and let your flesh and blood obey it.

Orsino. Well, I will be so much a sinner, to be a double-dealer: there's another.

Feste. Primo, secundo, tertio, is a good play, and the old saying is, 'the third pays for all': the triplex, sir, is a good tripping measure; or the bells of Saint Bennet, sir, may put you in mind; one, two, three.

Orsino. You can fool no more money out of me at this throw: if you will let your lady know I am here to speak with her, and bring her along with you, it may awake my bounty further.

Feste. Marry, sir, lullaby to your bounty till I come again. I go, sir, but I would not have you to think that my desire of having is the sin of covetousness: but, as you say, sir, let your bounty take a nap, I will awake it anon.   *Exit*

Viola. Here comes the man, sir, that did rescue me.

Enter Antonio and Officers

Orsino. That face of his I do remember well;
Yet, when I saw it last, it was besmear'd
As black as Vulcan in the smoke of war:
A bawbling vessel was he captain of,
For shallow draught and bulk unprizable,
With which such scathful grapple did he make
With the most noble bottom of our fleet,

That very envy and the tongue of loss
Cried fame and honour on him. What's the mat-
ter?
First Off. Orsino, this is that Antonio
That took the Phœnix and her fraught from
Candy;
And this is he that did the Tiger board,
When your young nephew Titus lost his leg:
Here in the streets, desperate of shame and state,
In private brabble did we apprehend him.
Viola. He did me kindness, sir, drew on my side;
But in conclusion put strange speech upon me:
I know not what 'twas but distraction.
Orsino. Notable pirate, thou salt-water thief,
What foolish boldness brought thee to their mer-
cies,
Whom thou, in terms so bloody and so dear,
Hast made thine enemies?
Antonio.   Orsino, noble sir,
Be pleas'd that I shake off these names you give
me:
Antonio never yet was thief, or pirate,
Though I confess, on base and ground enough,
Orsino's enemy. A witchcraft drew me hither:
That most ingrateful boy there by your side,
From the rude sea's enrag'd and foamy mouth
Did I redeem; a wreck past hope he was:
His life I gave him, and did thereto add
My love, without retention or restraint,
All his in dedication. For his sake
Did I expose myself, pure for his love,
Into the danger of this adverse town,
Drew to defend him, when he was beset:
Where being apprehended, his false cunning
(Not meaning to partake with me in danger)

Taught him to face me out of his acquaintance,
And grew a twenty years removed thing
While one would wink; denied me mine own
   purse,
Which I had recommended to his use
Not half an hour before.
Viola.   How can this be?
Orsino. When came he to this town?
Antonio. To-day, my lord; and for three months be-
   fore,
No interim, not a minute's vacancy,
Both day and night did we keep company.

Enter Olivia and Attendants

Orsino. Here comes the countess, now heaven walks
   on earth.
But for thee, fellow; fellow, thy words are mad-
   ness,
Three months this youth hath tended upon me;
But more of that anon. Take him aside.
Olivia. What would my lord, but that he may not
   have,
Wherein Olivia may seem serviceable?
Cesario, you do not keep promise with me.
Viola. Madam?
Orsino. Gracious Olivia,—
Olivia. What do you say, Cesario? Good my lord,—
Viola. My lord would speak, my duty hushes me.
Olivia. If it be aught to the old tune, my lord,
It is as fat and fulsome to mine ear
As howling after music.
Orsino.   Still so cruel?
Olivia. Still so constant, lord.
Orsino. What, to perverseness? you uncivil lady,
To whose ingrate and unauspicious altars

My soul the faithfull'st offerings hath breath'd out
That e'er devotion tender'd! What shall I do?

Olivia. Even what it please my lord, that shall become him.

Orsino. Why should I not, had I the heart to do it,
Like to the Egyptian thief, at point of death,
Kill what I love?—a savage jealousy
That sometimes savours nobly. But hear me this:
Since you to non-regardance cast my faith,
And that I partly know the instrument
That screws me from my true place in your fa-
vour,
Live you the marble-breasted tyrant still;
But this your minion, whom I know you love,
And whom, by heaven I swear, I tender dearly,
Him will I tear out of that cruel eye,
Where he sits crowned in his master's spite.
Come, boy, with me, my thoughts are ripe in mis-
chief:
I'll sacrifice the lamb that I do love,
To spite a raven's heart within a dove.

Viola. And I, most jocund, apt and willingly,
To do you rest, a thousand deaths would die.

Olivia. Where goes Cesario?

Viola.   After him I love
More than I love these eyes, more than my life,
More, by all mores, than e'er I shall love wife.
If I do feign, you witnesses above
Punish my life, for tainting of my love!

Olivia. Ay me, detested! how am I beguil'd!

Viola. Who does beguile you? who does do you
wrong?

Olivia. Hast thou forgot thyself? is it so long?
Call forth the holy father.

Orsino.   Come, away!

Olivia. Whither, my lord? Cesario, husband, stay.
Orsino. Husband?
Olivia.   Ay, husband: can he that deny?
Orsino. Her husband, sirrah?
Viola.   No, my lord, not I.
Olivia. Alas, it is the baseness of thy fear
   That makes thee strangle thy propriety:
   Fear not, Cesario, take thy fortunes up,
   Be that thou know'st thou art, and then thou art
   As great as that thou fear'st.

Enter Priest

                          O, welcome, father!
   Father, I charge thee, by thy reverence,
   Here to unfold, though lately we intended
   To keep in darkness what occasion now
   Reveals before 'tis ripe, what thou dost know
   Hath newly pass'd between this youth and me.
Priest. A contract of eternal bond of love,
   Confirm'd by mutual joinder of your hands,
   Attested by the holy close of lips,
   Strengthen'd by interchangement of your rings,
   And all the ceremony of this compact
   Seal'd in my function, by my testimony:
   Since when, my watch hath told me, toward my
      grave
   I have travell'd but two hours.
Orsino. O thou dissembling cub! what wilt thou be
   When time hath sow'd a grizzle on thy case?
   Or will not else thy craft so quickly grow,
   That thine own trip shall be thine overthrow?
   Farewell, and take her, but direct thy feet
   Where thou and I henceforth may never meet.
Viola. My lord, I do protest—

Olivia.   O, do not swear!
Hold little faith, though thou hast too much fear.

Enter Sir Andrew

Sir Andrew. For the love of God, a surgeon! Send
one presently to Sir Toby.

Olivia. What's the matter?

Sir Andrew. He has broke my head across, and has
given Sir Toby a bloody coxcomb too: for the love
of God, your help! I had rather than forty pound
I were at home.

Olivia. Who has done this, Sir Andrew?

Sir Andrew. The count's gentleman, one Cesario:
we took him for a coward, but he's the very devil
incarnate.

Orsino. My gentleman, Cesario?

Sir Andrew. 'Od's lifelings, here he is! You broke my
head for nothing, and that that I did, I was set on
to do 't by Sir Toby.

Viola. Why do you speak to me? I never hurt you:
You drew your sword upon me without cause,
But I bespake you fair, and hurt you not.

Sir Andrew. If a bloody coxcomb be a hurt, you
have hurt me: I think you set nothing by a bloody
coxcomb.

Enter Sir Toby and Clown

Here comes Sir Toby halting; you shall hear
more: but if he had not been in drink, he would
have tickled you other gates than he did.

Orsino. How now, gentleman? how is 't with you?

Sir Toby. That's all one: has hurt me, and there's the
end on 't. Sot, didst see Dick surgeon, sot?

Feste. O, he's drunk, Sir Toby, an hour agone; his
eyes were set at eight i' the morning.

Sir Toby. Then he's a rogue, and a passy measures
   pavin: I hate a drunken rogue.
Olivia. Away with him! Who hath made this havoc
   with them?
Sir Andrew. I'll help you, Sir Toby, because we'll be
   dressed together.
Sir Toby. Will you help? an ass-head, and a coxcomb, and a knave; a thin-fac'd knave, a gull?
Olivia. Get him to bed, and let his hurt be look'd to.
                    Exeunt Clown, Fabian, Sir Toby,
                                and Sir Andrew

               Enter Sebastian

Sebastian. I am sorry, madam, I have hurt your kins-
   man;
   But, had it been the brother of my blood,
   I must have done no less with wit and safety.
   You throw a strange regard upon me, and by that
   I do perceive it hath offended you:
   Pardon me, sweet one, even for the vows
   We made each other but so late ago.
Orsino. One face, one voice, one habit, and two per-
   sons,
   A natural perspective, that is and is not!
Sebastian. Antonio, O my dear Antonio!
   How have the hours rack'd and tortur'd me,
   Since I have lost thee!
Antonio. Sebastian are you?
Sebastian.   Fear'st thou that, Antonio?
Antonio. How have you made division of yourself?
   An apple, cleft in two, is not more twin
   Than these two creatures. Which is Sebastian?
Olivia. Most wonderful!
Sebastian. Do I stand there? I never had a brother;
   Nor can there be that deity in my nature,

Of here and every where. I had a sister,
Whom the blind waves and surges have devour'd.
Of charity, what kin are you to me?
What countryman? what name? what parentage?
Viola. Of Messaline: Sebastian was my father;
Such a Sebastian was my brother too,
So went he suited to his watery tomb:
If spirits can assume both form and suit,
You come to fright us.
Sebastian.   A spirit I am indeed;
But am in that dimension grossly clad
Which from the womb I did participate.
Were you a woman, as the rest goes even,
I should my tears let fall upon your cheek,
And say 'Thrice-welcome, drowned Viola!'
Viola. My father had a mole upon his brow.
Sebastian. And so had mine.
Viola. And died that day when Viola from her birth
Had number'd thirteen years.
Sebastian. O, that record is lively in my soul!
He finished indeed his mortal act
That day that made my sister thirteen years.
Viola. If nothing lets to make us happy both,
But this my masculine usurp'd attire,
Do not embrace me till each circumstance
Of place, time, fortune, do cohere and jump
That I am Viola, which to confirm,
I'll bring you to a captain in this town,
Where lie my maiden weeds; by whose gentle
   help
I was preserv'd to serve this noble count
All the occurrence of my fortune since
Hath been between this lady, and this lord.
Sebastian. (*to Olivia*) So comes it, lady, you have
   been mistook:

But nature to her bias drew in that.
You would have been contracted to a maid;
Nor are you therein, by my life, deceiv'd,
You are betroth'd both to a maid and man.

Orsino. Be not amaz'd; right noble is his blood.
If this be so, as yet the glass seems true,
I shall have share in this most happy wreck.
(*to Viola*) Boy, thou hast said to me a thousand
    times
Thou never shouldst love woman like to me.

Viola. And all those sayings will I over-swear;
And all those swearings keep as true in soul
As doth that orbed continent the fire,
That severs day from night.

Orsino.   Give me thy hand,
And let me see thee in thy woman's weeds.

Viola. The captain that did bring me first on shore
Hath my maid's garments: he upon some action
Is now in durance, at Malvolio's suit,
A gentleman, and follower of my lady's.

Olivia. He shall enlarge him: fetch Malvolio hither:
And yet, alas, now I remember me,
They say, poor gentleman, he's much distract.

Re-enter Clown with a letter, and Fabian

A most extracting frenzy of mine own
From my remembrance clearly banish'd his.
How does he, sirrah?

Feste. Truly, madam, he holds Belzebub at the
stave's end as well as a man in his case may do:
has here writ a letter to you; I should have given
't you to-day morning, but as a madman's epistles
are no gospels, so it skills not much when they are
deliver'd.

Olivia. Open 't and read it.

Feste. Look then to be well edified, when the fool delivers the madman. (*reads*) By the Lord, madam,—

Olivia. How now, art thou mad?

Feste. No, madam, I do but read madness: an your ladyship will have it as it ought to be, you must allow Vox.

Olivia. Prithee, read i' thy right wits.

Feste. So I do, madonna; but to read his right wits is to read thus: therefore perpend, my princess, and give ear.

Olivia. (*to Fabian*) Read it you, sirrah.

Fabian. By the Lord, madam, you wrong me, and the world shall know it: though you have put me into darkness, and given your drunken cousin rule over me, yet have I the benefit of my senses as well as your ladyship. I have your own letter, that induced me to the semblance I put on; with the which I doubt not but to do myself much right, or you much shame. Think of me as you please. I leave my duty a little unthought of, and speak out of my injury.   THE MADLY-USED MALVOLIO.

Olivia. Did he write this.

Feste. Ay, madam.

Orsino. This savours not much of distraction.

Olivia. See him deliver'd, Fabian, bring him hither.

Exit Fabian

My lord, so please you, these things further thought on,

To think me as well a sister as a wife,

One day shall crown the alliance on 't, so please you,

Here at my house, and at my proper cost.

Orsino. Madam, I am most apt to embrace your offer.

(*to Viola*) Your master quits you; and for your
    service done him,
So much against the mettle of your sex,
So far beneath your soft and tender breeding,
And since you call'd me master for so long,
Here is my hand: you shall from this time be
Your master's mistress.
Olivia.   A sister, you are she.

Re-enter Fabian, with Malvolio

Orsino. Is this the madman?
Olivia.   Ay, my lord, this same.
How now, Malvolio?
Malvolio.   Madam, you have done me wrong,
Notorious wrong.
Olivia.   Have I, Malvolio? no.
Malvolio. Lady, you have. Pray you, peruse that
    letter.
You must not now deny it is your hand:
Write from it, if you can, in hand or phrase,
Or say 'tis not your seal, not your invention:
You can say none of this: well, grant it then
And tell me, in the modesty of honour,
Why you have given me such clear lights of fa-
    vour,
Bade me come smiling, and cross-garter'd to you,
To put on yellow stockings, and to frown
Upon Sir Toby, and the lighter people;
And, acting this in an obedient hope,
Why have you suffer'd me to be imprison'd,
Kept in a dark house, visited by the priest,
And made the most notorious geck and gull
That e'er invention play'd on? tell me why.

Olivia. Alas, Malvolio, this is not my writing,
Though, I confess, much like the character;
But out of question 'tis Maria's hand.
And now I do bethink me, it was she
First told me thou wast mad; then cam'st in
    smiling,
And in such forms which here were presuppos'd
Upon thee in the letter. Prithee, be content:
This practice hath most shrewdly pass'd upon
    thee;
But when we know the grounds and authors of it,
Thou shalt be both the plaintiff and the judge
Of thine own cause.
Fabian.   Good madam, hear me speak,
And let no quarrel nor no brawl to come
Taint the condition of this present hour,
Which I have wonder'd at. In hope it shall not,
Most freely I confess, myself and Toby
Set this device against Malvolio here,
Upon some stubborn and uncourteous parts
We had conceiv'd against him: Maria writ
The letter at Sir Toby's great importance,
In recompense whereof he hath married her.
How with a sportful malice it was follow'd
May rather pluck on laughter than revenge,
If that the injuries be justly weigh'd
That have on both sides pass'd.
Olivia. Alas, poor fool, how have they baffled thee!
Feste. Why, 'some are born great, some achieve
greatness, and some have greatness thrown upon
them.' I was one, sir, in this interlude, one Sir
Topas, sir, but that's all one. 'By the Lord, fool, I
am not mad.' But do you remember? 'Madam,
why laugh you at such a barren rascal? an you

smile not, he's gagg'd:' and thus the whirligig of
time brings in his revenges.

Malvolio. I'll be reveng'd on the whole pack of you.

Exit

Olivia. He hath been most notoriously abus'd.

Orsino. Pursue him, and entreat him to a peace:
He hath not told us of the captain yet:
When that is known, and golden time convents,
A solemn combination shall be made
Of our dear souls. Meantime, sweet sister,
We will not part from hence. Cesario, come;
For so you shall be, while you are a man;
But when in other habits you are seen,
Orsino's mistress and his fancy's queen.

Exeunt all, except Clown

Feste. (*sings*)
When that I was a little tiny boy,
    With hey, ho, the wind and the rain,
A foolish thing was but a toy,
    For the rain it raineth every day.

But when I came to man's estate,
    With hey, ho, &c.
'Gainst knaves and thieves men shut their gate,
    For the rain, &c.

But when I came, alas! to wive,
    With hey, ho, &c.
By swaggering could I never thrive,
    For the rain, &c.

But when I came unto my beds,
    With hey, ho, &c.
With toss-pots still had drunken heads,
    For the rain, &c.

W·HEATH·ROBINSON

A great while ago the world begun,
   With hey, ho, &c.
But that's all one, our play is done,
   And we'll strive to please you every day.

Exit